DOWN EAST NURSE

DOWN EAST NURSE

Rose Dana

THORNDIKE
CHIVERS

This Large Print edition is published by Thorndike Press®, Waterville, Maine USA and by BBC Audiobooks, Ltd, Bath, England.

Published in 2004 in the U.S. by arrangement with Maureen Moran Agency.

Published in 2005 in the U.K. by arrangement with the author.

U.S. Hardcover 0-7862-7159-0 (Candlelight)
U.K. Hardcover 1-4056-3214-3 (Chivers Large Print)
U.K. Softcover 1-4056-3215-1 (Camden Large Print)

The text of this Large Print edition is unabridged.
Other aspects of the book may vary from the original edition.

Set in 16 pt. Plantin by Ramona Watson.

Printed in the United States on permanent paper.

British Library Cataloguing-in-Publication Data available

Library of Congress Cataloging-in-Publication Data

Dana, Rose, 1912–
    Down East nurse / by Rose Dana.
        p. cm.
    ISBN 0-7862-7159-0 (lg. print : hc : alk. paper)
    1. Nurses — Fiction. 2. Physicians — Fiction.
3. Maine — Fiction. 4. Large type books. I. Title.
PR9199.3.R5996D69 2004
    813'.54—dc22   2004056904

DOWN EAST NURSE

Chapter One

The old-fashioned farmhouse with its gray clapboards and narrow front verandah was perched on a hillside overlooking the small Maine town of Wellsport. The winding country road that served the outskirts of this fishing village and summer resort passed by the house as it snaked farther up the mountain until it reached the highest point and made its return to the town by a circuitous route. Julia Lee stood thoughtfully with an arm linked around the corner verandah post as she took in the view stretched out before her.

This lovely scene was the most vivid of all her childhood memories. At any time she could even now close her eyes and picture the rolling green lawn that reached to the road, and beyond it the descending fields of neighboring farmers with their herds of multi-colored cattle clustered usually in groups, the white, rambling farmhouses and the imposing barns. And far beyond all this, the distant pattern of white houses ranged neatly around a cove of blue water, the town of Wellsport. To the left was the big summer resort hotel, Manorview, whose stately yellow and white bulk dwarfed the town. This cluster of large buildings comprised a small city in itself, and to it each summer came hundreds of wealthy tourists to enjoy its stately pleasures. On a high point at the other end of the town was the red brick building where she spent her working days. The Dixon Memorial Hospital was not as large as the big summer resort, but as one of its nursing staff, Julia Lee felt it had much more importance.

Her father's voice broke into her thoughts. "The way you're staring at the town," he observed dryly, "you'd think you'd never seen it before."

Julia glanced at him, a smile on her attractive face. "I was just comparing the reality with my memory picture," she told him. "I don't believe I've ever forgotten a single detail."

Tom Lee chuckled. "One thing about Wellsport, it doesn't change in a hurry. Guess that's true of all this part of Maine." He was sitting at the other end of the verandah in an ancient rocking chair, a spare man of late middle-age, his sturdy features bronzed by the sun and his hair prematurely white. Dressed in rough work trousers and plaid, open-necked shirt, he was smoking his favorite long-stemmed black pipe. To the casual observer he looked like a typical Maine farmer, but he was far from that, as Julia knew. Before he'd come here to live on this place, he'd been a teacher in Boston, and he had his bachelor's degree to prove it.

She studied him affectionately with her clear blue eyes. "I must have been twelve when we came here," she said. She didn't mention that it was the spring after her mother had died. In the years since she'd seen time ease the pain in her father's eyes, and she had no desire to bring it back.

"Just twelve," he agreed placidly, puffing on his pipe.

It was the quiet time of early evening when the people on the farms rested briefly, their day chores ended and the night ones not yet begun. Julia was silent a moment, then said: "I was always fascinated by the hospital. Even then I wanted to be a nurse."

Her father nodded. "And now you're a good one."

She laughed. "I wish I felt as sure of that as you do. Anyway, I'm just as fond of

9

nursing as I thought I'd be. At least I'm happy in my work."

"That's the main thing," her father said.

She gave him a searching look. "Have you been happy here all these years? You've been alone since I went to nursing school and to work. Sometimes I think I should buy a car, and then I could drive back and forth to the hospital and live here with you."

Her father removed his pipe. "You'd soon change your mind after a couple of winter storms. I think it's best for you to board in town. Besides, you have a lot more young company this way."

Julia sighed. "Perhaps. But I worry about you."

Tom Lee looked pleased and shrugged. "I appreciate that. Guess I'd be upset if you didn't. But I get along here fine on my own. It's the sort of life I like."

She went over and sat on a bench near him. "You've never felt you'd like to take up teaching again?"

He shook his head emphatically. "No. Thoreau said it all as far as I'm concerned when he wrote: 'I went to the woods because I wished to live deliberately, to front only the essential facts of life, and see if I could not learn what it had to teach and not, when I came to die, discover that I had not lived.' I've learned in my years here, and I've found contentment."

Julia's pretty face took on a frown. "But you have so much ability. It seems awful to waste it on a scrub farm like this that gives you only a bare living. You could have made lots of money if you'd wanted to."

Her father gave her a concerned glance. "Sorry I didn't?"

She raised her eyebrows. "There've been a few times when I wouldn't have minded being a rich man's daughter."

Tom Lee looked sad. "It's only when you say that I'm sorry I haven't any money."

She laughed, got up and threw an arm around his shoulders. "But most of the time I'm glad I'm poor Tom Lee's daughter. You're the most independent man in Wellsport."

"That's a real compliment," he chuckled, "when you consider Maine has the most cussedly independent Down Easters of all."

Julie straightened up and glanced in the direction of the road. "Dave should soon be along. His patient can't be taking this much time."

The white-haired man's eyes regarded her with a twinkle. "Just how serious are

11

things between you and young Dr. Dave?"

She looked at her father and blushed as she protested: "We're just good friends!"

"You go out with him a lot."

"We happen to work in the same hospital," she said. "So we're thrown in each other's company a great deal. I like Dave Farren."

"What does his father think about it?"

"I doubt that he's even noticed us together." Julian sighed. "The senior Dr. Farren has only one interest, and it takes all his time. That is keeping the Dixon Memorial Hospital a going institution."

Tom Lee's bronzed face took on a cynical expression. "Bill Farren is a good doctor. He's worked hard for this town and the hospital, but he has a weakness. He runs the hospital, and his wife runs him!"

She gave a rueful smile. "I've heard that before, but do you really think you're being fair?"

Her father took a puff on his pipe. "Yes," he said at length, "I'd say I am. Emily Farren has never been satisfied with her position in this town. She's a climber, and she really gets going when the summer crowd arrive."

Julia knew that much of what her father was saying was true. Nevertheless she protested: "I don't think there's anything so wrong in being socially ambitious."

"Not if you keep it in perspective," Tom Lee said dryly. "Emily doesn't. And by the way, how does it suit her to have her doctor son running around with a scrub farmer's daughter?"

Julia said quickly: "Here comes Dave's car now!" And she ran down off the verandah to meet him, relieved that she didn't have to answer her father's awkward question.

Dave had the top of his green convertible down on this warm June evening, and he waved at her boyishly as he swung the car into the narrow gravel roadway that led up to the house. She went across the lawn and was by the car when it came to a halt.

"Sorry to keep you waiting," he said, sliding across the seat and getting out of the car. He was almost a head taller than she was, with wavy brown hair, friendly gray eyes in a square, determined face and an engaging smile.

"It didn't matter," she said. "I've enjoyed having the extra time with Dad." She linked her arm in his, and they strolled back up to the verandah.

Tom Lee had gotten to his feet, and now he greeted Dr. Dave with a broad smile.

13

"What have you been doing to poor old Henry?" he wanted to know.

Dave Farren grinned. "Not much. Arthritis isn't easy to treat, and he has a bad case. I'm trying paraffin baths now."

Julia's father showed interest. "Sounds like an old time remedy."

"In a way it is," Dave agreed. "But it's given a lot of relief in a good many cases, and the way Henry is suffering, I thought it would at least be worth a try. I took him up the ingredients tonight."

"How does it work?" Julia asked.

"I told him to take three or four pounds of paraffin wax and one pound of vaseline and melt it in a double-boiler, being sure to keep the paraffin away from the open flame, and cool it until a thin white coating appears on the top. Then it's ready for use, and he's to dip his hands in it until four or five coatings have been applied, being sure not to move the fingers. He should keep his hands in the wax for close to half an hour. Then he can remove his hands from the mixture and pull off the cooled wax like a glove."

"Sounds like a lot of trouble." Tom Lee laughed. "I hope it helps Henry."

The young doctor smiled in grim agreement. "Don't worry! He'll let me know

14

next time I go up there if it doesn't."

Julia turned to her father. "Do you see Henry often?"

"Not as often as I should," he said. "I must take a walk up to his place tomorrow night."

Dave glanced at his wristwatch. "Don't want to hurry you, Julia. But it is getting late. I still have one more call near town, and by then it will be time for the dance."

Julia nodded, and then to her father: "I'll see you get those groceries, Dad. They'll probably be by on tomorrow's delivery."

"No hurry," he said.

"There's nothing else?" she asked.

"Not a thing," he assured her. And to Dave, "Come back again soon. I'm not much troubled with company."

"Thanks, I'll do that," Dave promised, and they left, her father waving from the verandah as they drove off in the direction of town.

Dave gave her an admiring glance from behind the wheel, and she was glad that she'd worn the white summer dress which was one of her best. Her complexion was dark, and she tanned fairly easily. Even now her skin was an attractive brown, and the dress showed this off to advantage, with its short sleeves and low neck.

The young doctor said, "Somehow I can't see you in that farm on the hill."

The statement caught Julia off guard, and she stared at him in genuine surprise. "I don't follow you."

He shrugged. "You're so chic and up-to-the-minute, you strike me as the city girl type."

"Have you seen any city girl types?" Julia asked. "If so, you'll know it's no compliment."

"You know what I mean!"

"You mean I'm not the small town New England type." Julia laughed. "I don't think that's true, either. These regional descriptions don't apply any more. And I spent three years at nursing school in Boston."

Dave turned the car into the main highway; now the houses were more numerous and were built closer together. Huge old elms lined the highway on both sides, their branches almost meeting overhead.

"I'd like to set my sights higher than the Dixon Memorial Hospital," Dave said. "I suppose I'm wrong about that, too. But I'm kind of sick of the Dixons and their big summer hotel and Wellsport in general."

"My!" Julia said. "We are in a mood!"

16

He gave her a glance again, a frown wrinkling his forehead. "There's something feudal about this setup. It smacks of the Middle Ages, when there was a lord of the manor surrounded by his faithful peasants."

She laughed. "Even the name of their hotel bears that out — Manorview!"

He brought the convertible to a halt in front of a three-story frame house that had seen better days and was badly in need of paint. He reached for his bag on the floor beside her.

"Probably the reason they named it that," he said. "They're the power here, and they know it. Believe me!"

"You sound as if you'd had some experience with them."

"I have," he told her grimly. "I'll tell you about it later. Meanwhile, if you'll excuse me, I have to see a little lady on the third floor who is expecting her fourth blessed event. If you can call it that, with her husband out of work for six months of every year."

Julia watched him get out of the car and hurry across the sidewalk and into the somewhat run-down house.

When he reappeared, he smiled wearily. "The little mother-to-be is in no danger yet," he announced. "I'd say we can count on seeing the dance through." He headed the convertible into traffic again. "Was I long?"

She smiled at him. "I hardly knew the time was passing. You left me so much to think about."

Dave raised his eyebrows. "I didn't realize."

"You sounded so bitter," she said. "I mean about the hospital and things generally."

"The Dixon Memorial Hospital with all its fifty beds, its magnificent staff of nurses and aides and its truly fine operating room does not strike me as the end-all in medicine. I would like to go on to better things, say a fellowship at the Lahey Clinic."

"You are thinking big!"

"Why not? Some of the fellows in my class who had no more ability than I have made the grade in big clinics. I'd at least like to try."

"What's stopping you?"

He shrugged, his eyes on the road. "Dixon Memorial Hospital and my Dad."

"He doesn't want you to try a larger field?"

Dave said, "I can't say that he's ever taken a definite stand. But both he and

Mother seem to assume I'm perfectly contented here and could ask for nothing better than his job when he retires."

So that was it!

They were now driving away from the center of town in the direction of the Wellsport Country Club. The club was situated on the main highway in the direction of Portland and had the only good golf course in the county. Thus it was supported by the gentry of all the surrounding towns. In the summer it was extremely busy, but in other seasons its activity was limited. Tonight was to be the first of many dances scheduled during the resort season, but since the full complement of summer people had not yet arrived, Julia knew it would probably be sparsely attended.

Dave spoke again. "By the way, Mother is having a cocktail party for the Dixons tomorrow evening. Of course you're invited."

Julia regretted for a moment that she was on day duty. If she'd been working the three to eleven shift, it would have given her a good excuse. She knew that Dave forced his mother to invite her to these affairs, and in turn his mother made it as unpleasant as she could for Julia.

She said, "I don't know whether or not I

can come. I haven't anything to wear."

He shot a glance at her. "What about that dress you have on?"

"I've worn it to your mother's parties several times already," she replied. "I'd feel shabby in it."

Dave's stern young profile showed his annoyance. "I'm counting on you to come," he said. "There'll be other people there beside the Dixons, and I'd like you to meet them."

"We'll see," she promised vaguely.

The mere thought of meeting the Dixons again was slightly upsetting. All the older members of the family had died off, and the management of the big hotel was now in the hands of the surviving son and daughter. Edna Dixon, slim, blonde and haughty, was in her mid-twenties, while her brother Bill was in his early thirties, dark, good-looking and a widower with a little girl of seven. Julia remembered them both as sophisticated young people, with their yachts and sports cars, when she was just a gawky high school girl, earning extra money as a waitress in the dining room of the opulent Manorview House. Now she'd caught up with them and was more or less their contemporary.

Bill Dixon was the more pleasant of the

two. His little daughter rarely came to Wellsport, and Julia understood that she spent most of the summer in Connecticut with her late mother's family. Edna Dixon was a cold, supercilious sort of person and not at all popular with the townspeople in Wellsport. Julia wondered why she hadn't found a husband and decided it was probably because of her difficult disposition. Last year she'd noticed that the blonde Edna had paid a good deal of attention to Dave. Julia wondered if she'd continue to shower him with her attentions this summer.

Dave turned the car into the short paved road that led up to the country club and the parking area to the left of it. The club was a two-story white building with general offices and small rooms on the lower floor and the main ballroom and dining area upstairs.

He said: "It's possible the Dixons will be here tonight. They arrived about three days ago."

"I hadn't heard," Julia said.

He parked the car. "I've been talking to both of them," he said. He got out and opened her door for her. "I guess they had a good winter in Florida."

She knew he was referring to the Dixons'

winter project, a smaller hotel which they operated in the Palm Beach district.

She smiled at Dave as they entered the club. "I don't suppose I'd ever see these sacred precincts if it weren't for you."

"Nonsense," he said. "Any of the other fellows would fall over themselves to have you come with them."

Julia doubted this. Even though Wellsport was a small town, its social group was snobbish and kept its circle intact. It wasn't likely that the daughter of Tom Lee, a scrub farmer on the mountain road, would be invited, regardless of her personal charm. And certainly being a nurse at Dixon Memorial didn't make her one of the set. In fact, she was the only one of the nursing staff who attended the club regularly, thanks to Dave.

People were standing around in small groups when they entered. Dave checked his bag and her coat with an attendant, and they went into the largest of the lower floor rooms. Almost at once a man with horn-rimmed glasses, an eager oval face and wiry red hair that stood straight up from his head pushed forward, a glass in his hand. He was Ned Berry, the town druggist and mayor.

"Hello, kids!" He gave them a hearty

greeting that somehow seemed to Julia to ring false. "Nice to see you two take a little time off from the sick."

"We just manage." Dave smiled in return. "How's the mayor business?"

Ned Berry laughed. "Too busy filling out prescriptions to find out. And now that the social season's started, I guess I won't have any time for the Council at all." He surveyed the rapidly filling room with undisguised joy.

"One thing interests me, Mayor," Dave said. "I'd like to know what the Council thinks about that report I sent them."

Ned Berry swung back and stared at the young doctor somewhat guardedly from behind his thick glasses. "Oh, the report!"

"You did get it?"

The mayor nodded. "Yes, indeed. I remember it well. Read it to the others, and we talked about it." He nodded, a serious expression crossing the oval face.

"Did they come to any decision?" Dave asked.

The man with the horn-rimmed glasses ran a hand through his wiry red hair and looked thoroughly uncomfortable. "We decided," he said, "to wait and see what the Dixons had to say."

"Some decision!" Dave said impatiently.

The mayor was all innocence. "Don't know what else you expected us to do, Dave."

The young doctor gave a resigned sigh. "I thought you'd stand on your own hind legs and tell the Dixons what had to be done for a change."

Ned Berry laughed weakly and addressed himself to Julia. "This young man of yours is quite a joker, Julia."

"I'm not joking," Dave said sternly. "And you may find out the hard way. As things stand, this town is living on the edge of disaster."

The mayor looked distressed. "I don't think it's as serious as that. Mind you, Dave, I see it your way."

"But the Dixons are the ones who really own all of us, aren't they?" Dave's tone and expression were cynical.

The mayor became all ruffled dignity. "Now I can't have you saying things like that, Dave. Nobody owns me or any of the rest of the Council. We stand on our own two feet."

"And bray like frightened donkeys," Dave declared. "Sorry. I'm not impressed." And he took Julia by the arm and led her away.

She glanced up at him and whispered: "What was that all about?"

"Explain it later," he promised. "Just now we're about to be hailed by royalty."

Edna Dixon, blondely resplendent in a flashing crimson gown, stood with another couple directly in front of them. On seeing Dave, she broke into a delighted smile and came to meet him.

"Dave, darling! It's good to see you again!" She underlined the remark by taking him by the coat lapels and kissing him full on the lips in front of everyone in the room. Julia felt suddenly lost and out of things.

Chapter Two

Dave disengaged himself from the statuesque blonde as soon as he decently could without seeming to brush her off. He turned to Julia, his face red and showing embarrassment.

Then by way of introduction he said, "You must remember Julia."

Edna Dixon arched her eyebrows. "Why, yes, of course. The little nurse from the hospital. We met at your mother's one night."

Dave spoke quickly. "That's right. And I imagine you'll be seeing each other again at the cocktail party tomorrow night."

Julia felt it was time to say something. "I'm not sure yet that I can come."

Edna Dixon managed to look properly distressed. "But you must come, darling! Emily always gives the most divine parties."

Dave smiled. "She's been putting a lot of work into this one."

"There are so many things I want to tell you, Dave," Edna said, ignoring Julia and giving him an intimate look. "We must have some dances and talk."

"I'll count on that," he said with a touch of evasiveness in his tone. "I suppose Bill is here somewhere?"

"Find the prettiest girl and you'll locate him," Edna warned. And then to Julia, "I adore your dress, darling. It's so simple and plain."

"Thank you," Julia answered in a small voice. Edna had made it clear she thought the dress an inexpensive rag.

Dave brought the difficult conversation to a close. "We'll be getting upstairs," he said. "It's not often I get a free evening for dancing, and I want to enjoy every one."

Edna smiled. "I'll see you both later." And she turned again to the friends to whom she'd been talking when they first came up.

Julia and Dave quickly made their way to the broad flight of stairs that led to the second floor and the ballroom. As they climbed the stairs, she looked at him with a mischievous twinkle in her blue eyes. "You were given a rousing welcome," she said.

Dave shook his head hopelessly. "Edna doesn't improve. Each year she gets a little more brazen! I think she deliberately acted that way to embarrass us."

"In that case she scored one hundred percent!"

"What a vixen!" Dave's tone was one of awe.

The music had already started, and as they reached the ballroom floor quite a few couples were dancing to the lively music. Dave smiled at Julia and took her in his arms as they joined the other dancers. He was an excellent dancer and gave a strong lead. She found herself enjoying the evening for the first time. The awkward scene with Edna was forgotten, and she relaxed in his arms as they moved around the dimly lit room.

The number ended, and they applauded the orchestra and moved off by themselves to a deserted corner of the room. There was a table, and Dave pulled out a chair for Julia and then sat beside her.

He said, "That was fun."

She smiled at him. "I enjoyed it, too."

"We must do this more often," he said, "now that the busy season is under way. We should have plenty of fun this summer."

Julia gave him a teasing look. "I can almost guarantee that, with Edna around. You've got those dances with her to look forward to this evening."

Dave groaned. "Don't mention it! I

think I'll hide when she comes up here."

"She's really very lovely," Julia said. "I think you're just pretending."

He gave her a reproachful look. "It's not how she looks; it's the way she sounds! If she'd just relax and be herself, she'd be quite a gal! But she has to be so artificial."

"With her money she can behave as she likes," Julia reminded him.

"Maybe that's how she sees it, but I think differently," Dave said. "Let's not talk about her any more."

"If you like," she agreed. And changing the subject, "You seemed to have the mayor pretty worried."

Dave frowned. "Not worried enough, I'm afraid."

"Is what you were talking to him about a dark secret?" Julia wanted to know. "I ask because it's still all a mystery to me."

He smiled wanly. "No reason you shouldn't know the details. It's about the Wellsport sewerage system. I sent the City Council a letter pointing out the danger of the situation here."

She found herself immediately interested. "What sort of danger?"

"Pollution of the cove water, for one thing," he said.

"You mean the local sewerage system isn't adequate?"

He nodded. "That puts it mildly." Then, correcting himself: "Oh, it's all right for nine months of the year when our population is small. But then the three summer holiday months come around, and the system is hopelessly inadequate to cope with the strain of the swollen population."

Julia looked at him. "And this is the danger time from standpoint of possible epidemic."

"You've hit it exactly," he said, obviously impressed by the way she'd caught on. "A lot of people use the hotel swimming pool, but many of them still swim in the cove. And all the people from the camps and smaller hotels, including our own youngsters, use the cove. And the water is at the danger point of pollution."

"What's the answer?" she wanted to know.

"The Dixons will have to spend some money on the Manorview facilities, and the town should install a new sewerage plant and have the disposal pipes outlet beyond the cove."

"That means quite a lot of money," she said.

"It does," he agreed. "But I should think the taxpayers would rather have it than an

30

epidemic. That could be more expensive if the cost were counted in lives lost."

She stared at him. "You think it's that serious?"

"It's that serious," he said solemnly.

"What will you do if the mayor and the Council don't take any action?"

He shrugged. "I'll keep after him. I'll also take the matter up with the Dixons."

Julia smiled wryly. "I can't see the fastidious Edna giving much of an ear to sewerage problems."

Dave smiled in agreement. "Don't worry! This kind of stuff is looked after by their manager, Stephen Malcolmson. He's a tough one to deal with, too. More interested in Manorview profits than in spending money for safety measures. But I'll keep after him and the Council until they do something."

"And if they won't listen?"

"There's the State Health Board. I'll ask them to intervene."

She sighed. "Thereby making yourself the most popular young man in Wellsport."

"I'm not interested in popularity," he said flatly. "But while I'm practicing medicine here, I am interested in the health and safety of our people."

"I'll be interested in hearing what happens," Julia said.

"I'm glad. And meanwhile, don't do any swimming in the cove and warn any others who might be planning it that it's dangerous."

"I doubt if some of them will listen to me," Julia told him "They've been doing it for years."

He sighed. "That's the trouble. They don't seem to realize that with each passing year, the summer population has grown and the danger has increased as well."

The music began again, and they joined the other dancers. Julia found herself impressed by this serious side of Dave. He was plainly concerned by this situation and intended to try to do something about it, regardless of the cost to him personally.

The mayor danced by them with Edna Dixon in his arms. The blonde girl looked rather bored and unhappy.

Almost as soon as the music ended, she came up between them. With a glance at Dave, she turned to Julia and said, "Darling, I have something dreadfully personal I want to discuss with Dave. Would you be a dear and excuse us for a moment?"

Julia gave Dave a knowing, teasing look. "Of course," she said.

Edna needed no further permission. Before Dave could say a word, she took him by the arm and led him off to the other side of the room. Julia watched them disappear in the crowd gathered at the opposite side of the dimly lit ballroom and wished she hadn't been so generous.

Trying to be as inconspicuous as possible, she turned and made her way slowly to the table where she'd been sitting with Dave before the last dance. She sat down and hoped that he wouldn't be too long returning.

She had been there only a few minutes when she saw another male figure coming toward the table. He was dressed in a light summer suit, and his handsome face smiled as he bent slightly to ask, "How are you this evening, Miss Lee?"

She found herself surprised and pleased. It was none other than Bill Dixon, and he'd remembered her. She said, "Very well. It's nice to have you back again."

"May I?" he asked, indicating the empty chair beside her.

"I'd enjoy the company," she said.

He sat down, and his keen black eyes studied her. "You know you've grown into a really lovely young woman," he said. "I knew you when you were the proverbial ugly duckling."

This candid comment made her feel both flattered and embarrassed at the same time. She looked at him demurely. "I had no idea anyone paid that much attention to me."

He sat carelessly in his chair, an elbow resting on the back of it as he looked at her with friendly amusement. "I mean it. I've been watching you since way back."

"You make yourself sound like a very old man."

"I am a very old man," he said. "I'm the father of a seven-year-old daughter."

She nodded. "I know. Karen. She's a little beauty."

He showed interest. "You've seen her?"

"Last summer for the first time. In the garden at Dr. Farren's home."

Bill Dixon nodded. "Yes. We were there for one of Emily's endless parties." He gave her another of his magnetic smiles. "But we were talking about you."

"A dull subject."

"Not at all," he protested. "As I said, I remember you when. First, as a relish girl in the dining room at Manorview House."

She smiled agreement. "I worked there four summers, until I went to nursing school in Boston."

"I remember all four of them," Bill

34

Dixon assured her. "The first one you were long-legged, gawky and frightened speechless. The second you had just a little more grace. And it was during the third that I noticed you were filling out in the most interesting places and you'd learned to smile politely at the guests." He paused. "And the fourth year I realized that you were going to emerge as a real beauty. So I was waiting for you that fifth year, but of course you didn't come back."

"Were you very disappointed?"

He laughed. "Completely crushed."

"I'm sorry. I might have come back if I'd known. I thought no one was aware of anything but that tray of pickles." She closed her eyes. "I can see them now. Do you know I'm still not hungry for pickles to this very day?"

Bill laughed again. He said, "You see you are much too prosaic, while I'm a confirmed romantic."

Julia's eyes twinkled. "They tell me it's a difficult world for romantics."

"I know." He sighed. "But it's difficult to change one's nature. I should think Tom Lee's daughter would understand that better than most people."

She looked at him in surprise. "You know my father?"

"Longer than you think," he said. "When you were a very little girl, too young to notice boys, I used to hike through the woods with him. Once we shared a pet raccoon whose mother had been killed by a passing car. Your father is quite a man."

"I like to think so," she said. "Funny. He's talked about the hotel and you people, but he's never mentioned knowing you."

Dixon's face became sober. "Perhaps that's because he really doesn't know me today. He knew the boy I used to be."

"It was nice of you to tell me," she said quietly.

The young millionaire's face wore a thoughtful look. "Your Dad introduced me to Thoreau," he said. And then he quoted: "I love a broad margin to my life."

She smiled. "Weren't you a little young for Thoreau?"

"I don't think so." Bill Dixon eyed her pleasantly. "At least some of it got through to me then, and I had made his acquaintance to renew it from time to time as I grew older."

"Dad was always like that about his favorite authors," Julia agreed. "He had me reading Dickens and Mark Twain before I was ten."

Bill Dixon laughed. "Now that's what I call a father. I'm afraid I'm not doing as well by my Karen."

"She has a lot of time yet," Julia said.

He glanced around and said, "Don't tell me you came here by yourself."

She shook her head. "No. I came with Dave, or rather Dr. Farren. Your sister kidnapped him a few minutes ago."

"Poor young doc," Bill commiserated. "In that case he's really lost. I better plan to take you home."

Julia dismissed this suggestion with a light laugh. "I'm sure he'll escape in time for that chore."

"I'd consider it a pleasure and not a chore," he assured her. "It's been worth waiting to see you again. You're really lovely now."

She was beginning to feel he was making fun of her, teasing her as he would some forlorn youngster. With a growing uneasiness she glanced across the room in the hope of seeing some sign of Dave. And it was with real relief she at last saw him striding toward them.

She turned to Bill. "Here's Dave now!"

The tall young man rose as Dave came up to the table. He winked at the baffled doctor. "You should take better care of this charming girl," he warned. "I was on the point of stealing her from you permanently."

Dave smiled. "I realize the hazards."

Bill turned to her with a parting smile. "Until the next time, Miss Lee." And he left without waiting for a reply.

Dave sank weakly into the empty chair and gave her a knowing look. "That fellow is a fast worker."

"He is nice," she admitted.

"I thought I'd never get away from Edna," the young doctor groaned "She talks incessantly and never says a thing."

Julia smiled. "I'll bet you enjoyed every minute of it. You're pretending now just for my benefit."

Dave looked dismal. "If you believe me capable of that, you'll believe anything."

The music resumed, and they had another long dance together. Afterward Dave suggested that it was getting late and perhaps they'd better leave. Julia was quick to agree, since she was on day duty and had to be at work by seven. The dance was still in full swing when they left.

As they made their way to the car, Dave said, "I hope you didn't mind leaving this early. But I have an idea I'd better check on that mother-to-be again before I settle down for the night."

"I'm glad we didn't stay any longer," Julia said. And then, in a teasing tone: "After all, it's customary for Cinderella to leave before midnight!"

This nettled Dave. "Now what are you suggesting?"

"Not a thing!" She assured him with a small laugh.

But he didn't take the joke too well. She was soon sorry she'd teased him as he drove in a sulky silence nearly the whole way to her boarding place. She lived in a small house owned by a widow which was only a few blocks from the hospital. Dave parked the car by its front walk and studied her.

"Was it such an awful evening?" he wanted to know.

She leaned close to him and took his arm. "I had a wonderful time," she said softly. "I always enjoy myself when I'm with you."

He sighed. "You keep hinting you don't belong there, that you're not one of the crowd. Actually, you're too good for any of them."

Her eyes were bright with happiness as she gazed up at him. "As long as you think so," she said.

"I do." His tone was emphatic. Reaching

up a hand, he cupped her chin in it. Studying her with solemn eyes, he said: "Surely you know I'm in love with you."

She said, "Please, Dave, it's late!"

But he was persistent. "I do love you. And when I came back to that table tonight and found you with Bill Dixon, I was jealous."

She laughed lightly. "That's about the second time I've ever met him."

"And he seemed plenty impressed," Dave said. "How about letting me buy you one of those 'Private Property' rings with an extra big diamond so the message will be sure to get across?"

Julia shook her head. "Not yet, Dave. Maybe later."

"Why not now?"

"We both need more time to be sure."

"I'm sure enough now." And to underline this, he pressed his lips to hers in a long kiss.

Once in her own room, Julia turned on the light and quickly undressed. The next thing she was conscious of was the alarm giving out its belligerent signal that it was six a.m. and time to get up for work. She yawned and gave a little groan as she blindly groped for the small clock and switched the alarm off. A few minutes later she was on her feet and preparing to wash.

Mrs. Sarah Thomas was humming a rousing revival hymn as she hurried into the dining room with a tall glass of orange juice and placed it before Julia.

"You look drawn and pale, dear," the stout matronly woman said after inspecting her.

Julia gave a wan smile. She'd only just come downstairs and was still feeling sleepy. "We didn't leave the club until almost midnight," she said. "And it took a while to get home."

Sarah Thomas smiled knowingly. "I can well believe that, if the young men haven't changed since my day. Getting home was usually the longest part of the evening."

Julia laughed. "It wasn't that bad. But we did sit in the car for a while."

The matronly woman pointed a finger at her. "You should give up this hospital business and get yourself some nice easy office job," she advised. She had a round, jolly face and a rather large red nose. "You're not strong enough to be a nurse, dear."

Julia sipped her juice. "Maybe I'll surprise you. I feel all right. It's just that I always looked peaked in the mornings."

Sarah Thomas vanished and returned a few minutes later with hot cereal and toast.

41

She believed in serving hot cereal all year around, regardless of how warm it got. "Put something solid in your stomach," she told Julia.

Julia dutifully covered it with cream and sugar. There was no use arguing with Mrs. Thomas. Easier to eat whatever she put before you.

This morning the stout woman was eager for news. "Bet there was a big crowd at the dance," she said, standing with arms akimbo.

"A lot of people were there I didn't know," Julia told her. "Probably from some of the other towns. And of course the mayor was there."

"That pipsqueak," Mrs. Thomas said angrily. "Suit me better if he stayed home and tried to think of some way of lowering our taxes."

"From all I hear, they might get higher," Julia warned her.

Mrs. Thomas registered dismay. "You don't mean it! I'm paying more than I should on this old wreck now. What excuse would they have for raising the rates more?"

"Something to do with a new sewerage plant," Julia said. "I don't know whether it will go through."

"It better not," the landlady said grimly. "They've spent enough money as it is."

Seeing that she'd hit on a touchy subject, Julia tried to get the landlady's mind off it by telling her, "The Dixons were there, too, both of them."

It worked. Sarah Thomas became interested at once. "Were they now? I'll bet Miss Edna was dressed fit to kill!"

"She had a lovely gown," Julia said, and went on to fill the older woman in on the details.

Mrs. Thomas sighed. "Those Dixons are the real thing, Miss Julia. Real society! The kind we get in Wellsport only in summer. And then there's just a few of the top ones, and they stay at the Manorview. When I worked there as chambermaid, I remember —"

And Julia listened as Sarah Thomas went on interminably about her adventures when she had worked as a domestic at the big hotel.

Then Sarah escorted her to the door as usual and said, "You've got a nice young man in that Dr. David. He's like his father. They're both fine men and the best doctors we've ever had in Wellsport."

The morning air was brisk, and even at seven a.m. there was the promise of a

43

pleasant, sunny day. Julia moved quickly along the elm-lined streets, as she didn't want to be late reporting at the hospital. She knew what it was like to work the tiring night shift, and she didn't like to keep Head Nurse Grace Perkins waiting. It took her only a few minutes to reach the hospital grounds. At close range, the big red brick building was much more imposing than the view of it from the front verandah of her father's farmhouse suggested.

It had been built jointly by the town of Wellsport and father of Bill and Edna Dixon. Because the senior Dixon had contributed so much of the money for its construction, it had been named in his honor. He had also left a handsome bequest in his will for its upkeep. There were no outside frills, and the front entrance and steps were not impressive. But the rooms and wards were well furnished and comfortable, and in such vital areas of the hospital as the operating room and the O.B. department equipment was the best and latest. The local people were proud of their hospital as well they might be.

Julia quickly changed into her uniform and cap and went up to the desk on the second floor where both surgery and medical patients were looked after. The head nurse in charge of the night shift was waiting to go through the various patients' cards with her. It was a regular routine, and as soon as they'd exchanged greetings Grace Perkins sat and went through the files in her dry nasal twang.

When it was over, she glanced at Julia over her glasses and said, "Dr. William Farren wants to see you as soon he comes to the office. It's urgent. I was to be sure and tell you."

Julia glanced at the older nurse with puzzled eyes. "Have you any idea what it means?" she asked.

Nurse Perkins' face was blank. She sighed. "I'm afraid it's trouble."

Chapter Three

In the busy hour that followed, Julia forgot all about the message that she should see Dr. William Farren as soon as he came to his office. The responsibilities of head nurse on the day shift were many and varied. Although there were no operations scheduled for the morning, she did have two recent post-op cases to look after.

The two nurses on whom she depended most were Millie Randall and Jane Freeman. Millie Randall was a jovial middle-aged nurse whose overweight didn't prevent her from being one of the most efficient and hard-working nurses on the floor. She had a rather pretty, full face and chestnut hair that was turning gray. Jane Freeman was the exact opposite in type. Thin and with straw-colored hair that hung limply in a plain cut, she was about Julia's own age. But she was brilliant and had a sense of humor, that belied her sad face and woebegone manner.

It was Millie Randall who bustled up to Julia's desk with the first problem of the morning. "I wish you'd look in on the Jones woman in 208," she said. "I'm having trouble with her."

Julia looked up from a chart she'd been checking. "She's the little dark woman from Lincoln who had the thyroid operation?"

Millie nodded. "That's the one. She was a nervous wreck when she came in here, and she's worse now. She keeps wanting to see Dr. Daniels."

Julia smiled. "Did you explain that Dr. Daniels is not in the habit of coming to the hospital until afternoon unless it's an emergency?"

"I've tried everything," Millie grumbled. "But she just keeps going on in that hoarse voice of hers."

"I'll see what I can do," Julia said, getting up from the desk.

Martha Jones was the wife of a well-to-do merchant in Lincoln and so had one of the better private rooms on the second floor. Julia remembered that she was child-less and something of a neurotic. Of course this was understandable, since she'd been suffering from a thyroid condition which had a tendency to make its victims lose weight, suffer from extreme irritability and crying spells and tremble. Martha Jones showed all these symptoms.

Julia had served as scrub nurse on the morning Dr. Dave Farren had operated on the Lincoln woman. They were all tense, as often nodular goiter could be of a malignant nature. Happily, in the majority of cases this was not so.

The small dark woman lay on the operating table, completely unconscious from the general anesthetic administered to her by the hospital's competent anesthesia nurse, Louise Hawkins. Louise was small and precise in her ways and had taken several advanced courses in her specialty.

Julia stood by with an array of instruments, clamps and sutures ready as Dave slightly rearranged the towels around the field of surgery and made ready for the first incision that would start the operation. Old Dr. Daniels was assisting, since this was his patient. He eyed her from the other side of the operating table, a bent, gnome-like figure in his green cap, gown and mask.

Dave made a precise movement with the scalpel, and the operation was under way. Julia watched as he proceeded with cool ease. The thyroid gland surrounded the windpipe in the lower part of the front of the neck. She knew it to be one of the most important parts of the human body, since it regulated the manner in which food was turned into energy. It was normally composed of three lobes measuring more than two inches in diameter.

"There are the trouble-makers!" old Dr. Daniels rasped as Dave's scalpel revealed the thyroid and showed several pea-sized lumps on the organ.

It was only the work of minutes to remove the growths. Dave's eyes rose from the incision as he said: "None of the usual signs of a malignancy."

Old Dr. Daniels nodded. "I think we can safely proceed on that assumption. But as a precaution, see that the specimens are sent to Portland immediately."

After that, it was a matter of completing the procedure. An hour and a quarter from the time she'd been wheeled into the modern, well-lighted operating room of the Dixon Memorial Hospital, Martha Jones was being taken back to her room by the waiting orderlies, all stitches and clamps safely in place and the hazards of the operation over.

Dave removed his mask and smiled at Julia. "That didn't turn out so badly."

Dr. Daniels was at his side. "Don't forget about sending specimens to Portland," he warned again. "We have to be sure."

As it turned out, the word from Portland was good. The small growths were benign. This had all taken place five days ago, and Martha Jones should have been well on her way to recovery.

Julia went into 208 with Millie at her side. Martha Jones was sitting up in bed, and when she saw them her pinched features showed anger. "Have you phoned Dr. Daniels as I asked?" she asked in the hoarse whisper that had been her voice since the operation.

Julia moved close to the bed and smiled at the patient. "I thought Miss Randall explained that Dr. Daniels doesn't come to the hospital this early in the day unless there is a good reason."

"There is a good reason," Martha Jones said hoarsely.

"Perhaps if you'd explain," Julia suggested.

Martha Jones looked even more angry. "Listen to me!" she demanded. "Something must have happened in the operation. The surgeon bungled it, and now I have no voice."

Julia and Millie Randall exchanged a brief glance.

"I'm sure you're wrong," Julia told Martha Jones. "It's quite normal for you to have this hoarseness for several days."

The dark woman raised her eyebrows. "For five days?"

Julia sighed. "I think you're speaking much more normally than you were."

Millie Randall supported this, saying, "I've noticed that, too. And I've been looking after the patient since she first came in."

Martha Jones scowled at them. "You'd say that anyway."

"Not at all," Julia assured her. "I'd call Dr. Daniels if I thought it necessary. Dr. Farren will be here shortly, and I'll have him come and see you."

"I want to talk to Dr. Daniels when he comes this afternoon," the dark woman said, indicating by her tone she had little faith in Dave, even though he'd done all the actual surgery.

"I'll be sure and tell him," Julia said with a small professional smile. "In the meantime, try and relax. Your nervous condition could hinder your voice recovery. Just try to be patient."

She left the room and went back to her desk. The thin girl, Jane Freeman, was there. She greeted Julia with a bleak look.

"I had a few minutes free," the thin girl said. "So I've stayed here to take any phone calls."

"Anything important come in?"

Jane Freeman pointed to the scratch pad, "Dr. Dave Farren has a patient arriving about three o'clock. Suspicion of gallstones. He wants a private room for her."

Julia sat down and studied the scrawled message. "Mrs. Bates. I think she's a sister of the hardware dealer on Oak Street."

"Could be," Jane agreed listlessly. "How was the party at the country club last night?"

Julia smiled at the sad-faced girl. "Not bad at all. Both the Dixons were there."

Jane made a face. "So the summer gentry have arrived at last. What was she wearing?"

"Edna had on a grown of flaming crimson," Julia recalled. "It was striking."

"Anyone with her clothes and money can be attractive," Jane said. "She's really too thin and tall!"

Julia was amused. "I thought you were on the side of thin girls. After all, you are one yourself."

"Don't I know it!" Jane complained. "The only places I show any curves are where the ends of my bones push through the skin. And Edna isn't any better."

"Her brother is nice."

Jane looked skeptical. "I've heard some stories about him, too!"

Julia was interested. "Such as what?" she asked, studying the thin girl's face.

Jane seemed sorry she'd broached the subject. With an expression that showed embarrassment, she said, "Nothing too important. Maybe it was all lies, so I won't repeat it."

Julia was going to question her further, but at that moment the phone on her desk rang. She reached for it, and when she picked up the receiver she heard Dr. William Farren's crisp voice at the other end of the line. "I'm in my office now, Miss Lee," he said. "Could you manage to come down?"

Julia suddenly remembered the message the night supervisor had left with her. Probably she should have gotten in touch with him sooner.

She said, "I'll be down at once, Doctor."

As she put the phone down, Jane gave her a questioning look. "What's that all about?"

Julia was already on her feet. "Some front office problem. Will you cover for me here until I get back?"

Jane nodded. "Try not to be too long. I've got an intravenous to look after soon."

Dr. William Farren's office was located on the ground floor of Dixon Memorial to the right of the lobby and almost directly across from the information desk and switchboard. There was no one around but the girl sitting at the switchboard. She waved at Julia as the latter got off the elevator.

Julia smiled at her and went on to the half-open door of Dr. William Farren's private office. She tapped on the door and waited.

"Please come in," the older Farren's crisp voice commanded her.

She stepped inside, and he rose from behind his dark desk and waved her to a chair. "Please sit down, Miss Lee."

As she did so, he moved toward the door and shut it before resuming his seat behind the desk. "Now about my reason for asking you here," he began.

"Oh, yes," she said, and waited.

The senior Farren looked grave. "This is not something I want to get around," he said. "I must ask you to promise to keep what I tell you strictly confidential."

Julia found herself becoming more curious every minute. "Of course," she said.

He studied the top of his desk, seeming not to want to look directly at her. "There have been some thefts in the hospital," he said. "Serious thefts."

She found herself surprised and awkward. She hadn't expected anything like this and found it difficult to make an answer.

At last she said, "On my floor?"

"I'm afraid so, Miss Lee."

"What sort of thefts?"

Now he raised his eyes to meet hers. "Narcotics, Miss Lee. Someone has been pilfering from the drug supplies."

She frowned. It seemed incredible. "But we keep a careful count of everything. Each head nurse checks after her shift and transfers the keys to the incoming nurse."

"I'm well aware of the procedure," the balding doctor said curtly. And then, as if regretting his tone, he went on, "Please don't get the idea I'm accusing you personally. In fact, most of the shortages have occurred between the relief shift and the all-night one."

"I see," Julia said. "Then someone on the three to eleven shift must be the thief."

He nodded agreement. "I'm forced to that conclusion." Another pause. "Of course someone with a key to the drug cabinet could come by during those hours and take the stuff."

"Naturally you'll change the lock," she said.

"We're doing that immediately," he agreed, "on the theory that someone has managed to make a duplicate of one of the keys; someone with no right to such a key. But I believe there will be further attempts made to steal drugs even after this is done. So I want you to keep a careful eye out for suspects."

Julia smiled uneasily. "There's not much I can do beyond taking the usual precautions."

"Keep an eye open for any suspicious actions on the part of any of your staff," Dr. William Farren told her. "The culprit has to be someone in the hospital. If you notice anything that seems to have the slightest bearing on this matter, I want you to notify me at once."

"I will, sir," she promised.

"That is all, Miss Lee," he said by way of dismissal. He stood behind his desk. "A locksmith will come sometime today and change the lock, and you will be issued new keys."

Jane Freeman gave Julia a weary glance as she returned. The thin girl said, "Did he read the riot act to you?"

Julia smiled. "It wasn't too bad. Just a matter of policy."

Jane got up. "That's one thing they're never short of here — new rules! I'd better get back to my patient and check that intravenous tube." She hurried away.

Again Julia found herself besieged with demands on her time. Dave arrived with plates on a patient who'd been entered with suspected disc trouble. They had given him an injection the previous day and taken myelogram X-rays of the spine after the opaque substance had been injected into the spinal canal. Now Dave showed her a positive myelogram, one which noted an obstruction deformity in the area of the spine where a herniated disc was suspected.

"That makes the diagnosis certain," Dave said. "Jameson has a slipped disc."

"If he needs an operation, it will mean Portland or Boston," Julia said. She knew that Dave did no neurological surgery.

His pleasant young face took on a look of frustration as he leaned against the desk. "Not that I wouldn't like to try a disc one of these days," he said. "But that means a year or two of specialization. It's not for this G.P."

Julia knew this was a sore spot with him. She said, "Are you certain he needs an operation?"

"I'd like to try traction and bed rest first," he said. "How has he been this morning?"

"He complained during the night and was given heavy sedation," Julia said. "I don't think the full effects have worn off. He certainly hasn't been bothersome since I came on duty."

Dave gave her a teasing smile. "Well, now the situation is going to change. I'll need some help to get him in traction."

Julia sighed. "I'll call Millie Randall. She's experienced in that, and she has plenty of strength."

"Nurse Randall by all means," he agreed. "And you as well. Maybe Jameson will be happier when we tell him he has an eighty percent chance of being cured without an operation."

"Not if he knows he has to stay in traction for up to ten days." She smiled at the young doctor. "I don't think you'd like the prospect of being stretched on a rack for that long."

Jameson, who was a sturdy lobster fisherman with a loud voice and a generous supply of salty epithets to fit any drastic situation, accepted the traction quite meekly. Dave convinced him it was his best hope of getting well, and his spirits were buoyed by the thought that he wouldn't have to go through an operation.

Another crisis settled, Julia made the rounds of the other patients with the young doctor. Only in Martha Jones' room did they encounter outright hostility. The dark woman was still certain she was the victim of a botched job of surgery, and she made no bones about telling Dave so.

"Listen to me!" she complained. "I talk like a frog!"

Dave smiled. "Talk it over with Dr. Daniels. I'm sure he'll tell you just what we have. You're getting well fast, and your voice will gradually come back to normal."

"He's a doctor, same as you," she said sulkily. "Of course you back one another up."

"You should know that Dr. Daniels isn't that kind of man," Dave told her sharply, "if you know anything about him at all. What's given you this nonsensical idea that we might have damaged a vocal nerve and harmed your voice?"

"I read it in a doctor's book," the woman in the bed challenged him. "It said it happened a lot."

"Doctor's book!" Dave gave Julia a grim look. And then, turning to the patient: "I would hate to tell you the harm that comes of lay people reading all sorts of interpretations into what they find in doctors' books. I sometimes think it would be better if none of these so-called popular medicine books were printed and sold."

"A person has a right to know," Martha said belligerently.

"You have a right to proper information," Dave corrected her. "But it's idiotic to try to diagnose your own case from any medical manual. It takes a great deal more than reading to manage that. It so happens that I used the scalpel that cleared the growth from your throat. I know exactly what happened in there, and I can assure you no nerve was damaged." He turned on his heel and stalked out of the room.

Martha Jones stared after him with her mouth agape. Then she told Julia in her hoarse whisper: "How dare he talk to me like that?"

Julia said, "He's only thinking of your own good. Dr. Farren doesn't want you worrying yourself without reason. Everything he told you was true."

The dark woman was still fuming. She said, "Wait until I tell Dr. Daniels!"

Julia decided there was nothing to be gained by staying with her any longer, so she left the room, too. In the corridor, she found Dave waiting and consulting a brochure he'd taken from his pocket. He put it away and shook his head.

"That was a lovely exhibition," he said.

Julia shrugged. "In the long run, I think she'll benefit from what you told her."

"I sometimes wonder if anything helps in cases like that," he said. "Let's finish going the rounds."

They went in to see elderly Mrs. Molloy, who was past eighty and had broken her hip. With modern treatment it seemed likely she would walk again.

The old woman was a pleasant contrast to the intense Martha Jones. She smiled from the bed and asked, "How much longer, Doctor?"

"I'm not sure yet," he told her. "But you are doing well, and you'll be able to walk on your own before you know it."

The wrinkled old face brightened. "Will I need crutches or anything like that?"

Dave laughed. "Maybe we can settle for a cane. We'll get you a fancy one with a silver head."

This seemed to please the old woman. "I remember my grandmother had a cane," she recalled. "She used to point it at us children and scare us."

Dave winked at Julia. "Maybe I should

get one and use it on some of my patients."

So they finished their rounds on a happy note. Dave reminded Julia about the patient arriving in the afternoon and suggested they have lunch together in the cafeteria. She usually went down promptly at twelve.

After he'd gone, she brought the various charts up to date and marked the changes he'd suggested in medications. Since there were only three attending doctors at Dixon Memorial, she found herself on a very personal basis with all of them. She could almost predict the palliatives they'd recommend in certain cases or the treatments they would apply for various conditions.

As she finished this task, Millie Randall came up to the desk and glanced at the clock. A smile came over her broad face. "Just about time for your lunch, Julia. Especially if you want to meet your boy friend."

Julia blushed as she got up. "That's neither professional nor true," she said. "Dr. Farren is not my boy friend."

"Well, whatever he is, you'd better hurry down there, or he'll be tired waiting," Millie said without a sign she had been rebuked.

Julia gave her a hopeless smile and took the elevator down to the basement where the hospital cafeteria was located. It wasn't a large room and catered to both the staff and visitors. The area was divided by a latticed partition, and on one side of it there was a line of booths and a waitress to serve outsiders. When it was not busy, she and Dave often sat in one of the booths.

He was waiting in the corner one as she came in. He got up, and she smiled and went over and joined him. Almost at once the waitress took their order; then they sat back and relaxed.

Julia looked at him with twinkling eyes. "Millie Randall was afraid I'd keep you waiting."

He showed surprise. "It seems she knows our habits pretty well."

"This isn't a large hospital," she reminded him. "And doctors and nurses who lunch together are noticed."

He shrugged. "I don't mind. Do you?"

She smiled. "I guess not. Keeps the gossips from being frustrated."

"What are you going to wear to Mother's party tonight?"

She hesitated. "I'm not even sure I'm going."

"You'll have to come," Dave said seriously. "I've already told Mother that you'll be there. And Dad expects you as well."

She gave him a cynical glance. "I can just imagine your mother cheering at the news. I'll bet it made her day."

Dave looked hurt. "You don't understand her, Julia."

"That's what frightens me," she corrected him. "I'm sure I understand her only too well."

"It will be fun. Everyone is coming."

"Including Edna Dixon?"

"Especially Edna Dixon," he grinned, "and her charming brother. That should make it appealing to you."

She considered. "Well, he is the nicest millionaire I've ever known."

Dave raised his eyebrows. "You talk as if you'd known a lot of them!"

"Dozens!" she told him airily, and then broke into laughter.

He looked relieved. "For a minute you had me worried."

The waitress brought their food. Julia had chosen a fresh fruit salad, and Dave had settled for grilled ham and eggs.

After they'd started the meal, he said, "I understand you had a talk with my father this morning."

She looked at him across the table. "Yes.

64

I understood it was to be kept top secret."

He smiled. "Not from the staff. It's a nasty situation."

"Very nasty," she agreed. "I'll be glad when they find out who the thief is."

"Will you?"

She found his question puzzling. "Of course. It will be a relief to all of us. Why shouldn't I be glad?"

His face became grave. "I think that will depend on who the thief turns out to be."

Chapter Four

Julia returned to work at her desk on the second floor, and at exactly two-thirty the elderly Dr. Daniels made his appearance. He hobbled out of the elevator and made his way over to her.

"How are all my guinea pigs today?" he asked. It was his standard question.

She laughed. "Most of them are behaving themselves nicely. But I'm a little worried about Mrs. Jones. She seems in a difficult state of mind."

The wizened old face took on a scowl. The gray head bent to one side, and he said, "Tell me exactly what's been happening."

She did, finishing with the scene between his patient and Dave. She added: "I think Dr. Farren was justified."

The old physician nodded assent. "Bluntness is sometimes an excellent tonic for neurotics. I'll have a talk with that little lady myself." And he hobbled off down the corridor toward her room.

Nurse Jane Freeman came up to Julia,

the thin face showing more than usual worry. She said, "I saw Dr. Daniels going down the corridor. You better tell him to give special attention to Mrs. Myles, his diabetic case. She seems very uncomfortable today."

"I'll tell him," she promised.

"I don't like the look of her foot," Jane Freeman added before she left.

Julia knew what she meant. Mrs. Myles had an advanced case of diabetes which had brought on premature arteriosclerosis. Very likely the main artery in the troublesome leg was almost closed and the circulation so impaired that there was a real danger of gangrene.

It wasn't long before Dr. Daniels came hobbling back up the corridor. He wore a grim smile as he came close to Julia. "You won't have any more trouble from her," he promised. "She's making fine progress, and I told her so. I said if she caused any more trouble, I'd cross her off my patient list."

Julia laughed. "That should do it."

The old man chuckled. "It really seemed to worry her, though if she had any sense at all, she'd know it didn't matter. I won't be around many more years to doctor anyone."

"You shouldn't talk like that," Julia said. "You're good for at least another decade."

So the day continued. Before Julia left the hospital, she had taken a major part in making arrangements for Mrs. Myles, the woman with diabetes and gangrene complications, to be transferred to a Boston hospital, and she'd entered Mrs. Bates for observation as a possible gallstone case. When it came time to turn over the charts and keys to Laura Britt, the head nurse of the relief shift, she found herself tired and glad to be rid of the long day's responsibility.

Laura was a few years older than Julia and shared a cottage with a brother who divided his time between Maine and Florida. He was interested in racing in some way that Julia was not clear about. Laura was always evasive, but she hinted that he had a share in a stable. Julia felt it might have to do with the gambling end of the sport but preferred not to ask questions.

When she gave Laura the keys to the drug cabinet, the red-haired girl smiled wanly. She said, "I suppose you've heard about my trouble?"

Julia nodded. "Yes."

Laura's pretty face was pale. "I don't understand it. I'm frightened."

"I'm sure it will be all right now that Dr. Farren is aware of what's been going on," Julia said. "Just be careful."

"Believe me, I will." Laura sighed.

It was a bright sunny afternoon, with a tang of salt sea air such as could be found at its best only in Maine. Julia walked briskly, enjoying every minute of it.

Sarah Thomas was busy over the kitchen stove when Julia came in, and there was the pleasant aroma of cooking strawberries in the large old-fashioned kitchen. The buxom woman turned to her with a smile.

"Making my second batch of preserves today." She beamed. And trotting across to the big kitchen table, she picked up a spoon and dipped it into one of the filled bottles of preserves set out with their ruby red contents to cool. She came back to Julia and proudly offered her the spoonful of preserves.

Julia took the spoon and tasted the strawberries. "Wonderful!" she said. "I don't know how you manage to make them taste so good."

"Let's hope the judges at the fair feel the same way," Sarah Thomas said. She nodded toward the preserves on the stove. "This second lot will be better."

"Certainly smells heavenly," Julia said,

moving toward the stove and studying the bubbling strawberries as they cooked.

"Last year at the fair I won every one of the preserve prizes except the blackberry," Sarah Thomas said proudly. "And this year I'm after that, too!"

After a few minutes' talk, Julia went upstairs and threw herself full length on the soft feather mattress to rest a few minutes. Closing her eyes, she considered her day and the evening ahead. She had a premonition that going to the Farrens' parry would only bring her misery. But Dave seemed determined that she should go.

If she did, she had to decide what to wear. Her white dress was out, and that left only a red chiffon cocktail gown and a yellow one she'd just bought and would have to hem. She decided to wear the red, since it wasn't likely that Edna would show up again in the flaming crimson number she'd worn the night before.

Dave phoned after six and said he'd pick her up at eight. As soon as she finished dinner, she took a bath and dressed. By the time she finished with her hair, it was getting close to eight. She hurried downstairs and had Sarah Thomas hook up her back zipper.

The buxom woman stood back and admired her. "You're as slim as I was at your age," she said, her hands clasped her ample bosom.

Julia laughed. "You're so nice as you are, I can't imagine you being this thin."

"I was," the older woman insisted. "Before I married, my waist was as small as yours." This was a cue for her to begin a recital about all her young men and the good times they'd had. It went on until Dave arrived and rescued Julia.

When they drove up to the modern ranch style house that Emily had had built to her specifications only a few years back, Julia saw that a number of cars had gotten there before them.

She glanced at Dave, who was looking very handsome in black tie and white dinner jacket. "Quite a turnout," she said.

He pulled the car to an empty space near the back of the house and parked. "Some of them were here before I left to pick you up."

Dr. William Farren and Emily were receiving at the door. When it came Dave's and Julia's turn, the elder Dr. Farren took the nurse's hand and held it for a moment as he expressed his warm pleasure in seeing her. She had the feeling that he really was glad to see her. Not so when she faced his wife. Emily's thin, faded face took on an expression of bored friendliness.

"Oh, yes, of course I remember you. The little girl from the hospital," she said, not even attempting to call Julia by name.

Dave said, "Of course you know Julia." He put an arm lightly around her shoulders. "I've had her here plenty of times."

Emily looked pained. She said, "David, I do wish you'd straighten things out at the bar. I've been having trouble with that man from the hotel we hired to look after it. He seems to have everything in the wrong place." Without making any excuse or apology, she took Dave by the arm and literally dragged him off toward the far end of the big living room.

Dave turned to lift a hand and say, "I'll be right back, Julia."

Julia nodded and managed a smile. Then she turned to his father. But Dr. Farren was engaged in greeting some guests who'd just arrived. Feeling awkward and in the way, Julia moved into the living room area. All around her there were small groups standing talking. The party was surely a success, she thought grimly, but not for me.

"Hello again," a friendly voice said at her shoulder.

She turned and found herself staring up into the handsome face of Bill Dixon. He was holding a glass in one hand and looking relaxed and at ease with the world. "You look too solemn," he said. "Let me get you something."

Julia smiled. "I'm thirsty. I would appreciate a Coca-Cola with ice."

He raised his eyebrows. "Ice and nothing more?"

She nodded. "I don't need a drink, but I am thirsty. Coke and ice will fill the bill nicely."

"Be back in a minute," he promised.

She watched the tall young man delicately elbow his way through the crowd and felt better almost at once. He was as good as his word. It couldn't have been more than two or three minutes before he came back with her drink.

She took it and sipped from the cool glass. "Nice," she murmured.

He studied her with an amused expression. "I take it you're with Dr. Dave again. No other man could possibly be stupid enough to leave you alone like this. And I know he's done it before."

"His mother needed him at the bar," Julia said. "Some crisis, I understand."

Bill Dixon nodded toward the bar with a

cynical smile. "Some crisis is right. Do you know who's serving drinks there now? Dave and my sister Edna."

Julia couldn't help peering down the crowded room to see for herself. And sure enough, as shoulders parted she caught a glimpse of Dave and Edna gaily at work pouring out drinks while a short, fat man stood uneasily behind them. They had plainly taken over the regular bartender's chores.

Satisfied with what she'd seen, she turned back to Bill. "It seems he's just another victim of the dubious Dixon charm," she said with a shrug.

"Now wait a minute." The tall dark man laughed. "I don't like that dubious tag. Either we're charming or we aren't."

Julia was determined to tease him. She wrinkled her nose. "I suppose it's all a matter of taste."

"And you don't approve of us?"

"Well, maybe not entirely."

"Spoken like an honest Wellsport citizen," he agreed. "You know most of the townspeople don't like us at all. They think we come here in the summer to show off and make money on them." He paused and studied his glass. "Actually, it isn't that way at all," he said in a more serious tone.

"I have deep roots in this place. It represents a sort of haven for me, and I like the people."

His sincerity touched her to such a point she dropped her mask of disdain. "I'm sure many of them feel the same way about you."

He raised his eyebrows. "Well, that's a sudden change."

"Not really," she said with a sigh. She glanced toward the bar once more. "I was just indulging myself in a little pique with Dave and your sister. And I took some of it out on you."

The tall man stared at her. "I like your frankness."

"And I like your sincerity," she said. Taking in the chattering groups in the now overcrowded room, she added, "I'm sure there's not much of it here."

"I detest cocktail parties," he admitted. "Would I be committing an act of ingratitude toward my hosts if I suggested we get out of here?"

She finished her drink. "I doubt if they'd notice we'd left."

Bill looked wise. "Dave will notice soon enough, once he gets out of Edna's clutches."

Julia looked up at the tall man slyly.

"You think he'll be upset if he finds I've left?"

"He'll be badly upset!"

"Then let's go!"

It was settled as easily as that. They went out by the glass doors that opened on the patio. Julia got a last glimpse of Dave still at the bar, and she thought he looked a lot less happy than before, although Edna was laughing gaily as she passed out glasses.

The air outside was cold by contrast to the overheated room. Julia shivered, and Bill quickly opened her coat, which he'd been carrying, and draped it over her shoulders.

She looked up at him gratefully. "That's better."

He smiled. "And don't worry about the party. You're not burning any bridges. We can always go back, and no one will guess we ever left."

She strolled along under the trees. "Maybe I don't want that."

"You'd prefer to have Dave worry some?"

"I think he should realize his responsibilities," she said firmly. "And they're not all to his mother."

Bill kept step with her as they walked slowly toward the main road. "I know just

76

what you mean," he agreed. "If I were going to be Emily's daughter-in-law, there are some things I'd want to have settled."

Julia stared ahead, not wanting to look at him at the moment. "What makes you so certain I'm planning to marry Dave?"

"I just took it for granted."

"That isn't always smart."

He laughed. "I know. I only do it once in a while, when the odds seem very sure. Of course I could be wrong about you two." His voice became serious again. "And while we're on the subject, I might as well admit I think Dave is a nice fellow. There's not a thing I can say against him as a person."

Julia gave him a bitter smile. "Your sister seems to share your enthusiasm."

"Don't worry about Edna," he cautioned her. "She's no competition. When Dave really gets to know her better, he'll realize how much she is like his mother, and he'll start running in the opposite direction."

Julia said, "I've heard of men who didn't find out the truth until after they married."

"In which case," Bill said, "it serves them right for being so stupid." He stopped by a slim blue hardtop. "This is my car. How about a drive down to the hotel? We aren't opening officially until next week, but everything is ready, and I'd like to show you around."

"It sounds like a fine idea," she said.

"At least there'll be no crowds," he promised.

The drive to the hotel took less than ten minutes.

Bill Dixon parked the car in the paved driveway near the entrance. He glanced at Julia for a moment before attempting to get out. "I know what you're thinking about," he said, "and I wish you wouldn't. Let's leave all that unpleasantness behind and enjoy these few minutes together."

She smiled at him in the dim interior of the car. "That's a bargain," she said.

"Now I'll show you around," he said. And he went over and opened the door for her.

As they walked up the wide cement steps that led to the bank of glass doors, Julia said, "I must know this place as well as you do. I was a waitress here for four summers."

He laughed. "You've never seen it as a guest. Makes a big difference."

"That's probably all too true," she agreed.

So he gave her a grand tour of the place. And it was true that now she did see it

78

with different eyes. They paused in the ballroom under the ornate glass chandelier that he told her his father had bought in Vienna when the furnishings of one of the famous old palaces were being sold.

"Not so long ago," he said quietly, "men in bright uniforms and lovely women in flowing gowns danced gracefully under it. Perhaps their reflections are still caught magically in its prisms of glass, held there in an enchanted fashion all down the years."

There was a moment of silence, and Julia could almost visualize the graceful dancers of another era as they swirled to a gay waltz. She spoke at last. "Thank you for allowing me to share your thoughts. Somehow I feel I'll always remember this moment."

He lowered his eyes to meet hers, and his hands touched her shoulders. "It's a moment I'll always remember, too."

And with a mutual compulsion they came into each other's arms.

When the kiss ended, she moved away from him and went to stand by the window. Her eyes fastened on the reflected room in the silver waves. He came across to her, and they stood in the darkness, silent and full of wonder.

At last he said, "What happened just now, I didn't think it was possible." He paused. "I've lived so long with my hurt, covering what I really felt with a cold shallowness, that I didn't think I could ever sincerely feel love again."

"Don't!" she protested in a small voice. "It didn't mean anything. It was just a romantic incident. Blame it on the chandelier!"

His arm went around her. "Whatever I blame it on, I know I'm in love with you, Julia." And he drew her to him and kissed her again, a kiss of long, lingering intensity.

She broke away from him. "I think we should go back to the party now."

"Do you really want to go?"

Julia managed a smile. "We'd better."

"What about us?" There was pleading in his tone.

"Let's see if this survives the sunlight," she suggested.

"I'm not worried about that," Bill told her. "But you do puzzle me. Why are you afraid of falling in love with me?"

It was another of his direct questions. She smiled again. "Maybe there's a lot more of that frightened little waitress with the pickle tray still in me than you realize. Tonight will take some time for me to get used to."

"This is another world, Julia," he said earnestly. "We're different people now."

"I wonder," she said. And then, "Please let's hurry back. Dave will be in a raging mood."

Chapter Five

After the upsetting events of the previous evening, Julia was not surprised when a dramatic sequence of happenings brought her beside Dave Farren at the operating table of Dixon Memorial Hospital the next morning.

She received the first hint of what was ahead when she took over from Head Nurse Grace Perkins of the night shift. After she'd finished with the patients' files and received the various keys, the prim night supervisor told her about the emergency.

"There's been a bad car accident over Lincoln way," Grace Perkins told her. "The driver of one of the cars has fractures of both legs. They're bringing him here now."

"Has a doctor seen him yet?" Julia asked.

"Dr. Daniels lives near there," the head nurse of the night shift said. "He's coming with him."

Julia felt a sense of relief. If the veteran Dr. Daniels was with the injured man and had given the diagnosis, it was undoubtedly correct. She asked, "There's just one patient coming?"

"He was the only one hurt badly enough to need hospital attention. A wonder, too, from what I've heard." The prim nurse sighed. "I guess both cars are wrecks."

"If the fractures are serious enough, we'll be using the O.R.," Julia said. "I'd better make sure everything is ready."

Grace Perkins nodded. "That's right. And Dr. Dave Farren has been notified and should be here at any minute."

By the time Julia had made a hasty trip to the spotless pastel green operating room, seen everything was in readiness and returned to her desk on the second floor, young Dr. Farren had arrived.

"Has the accident case gotten here yet?" he asked Julia.

"Not yet," she said.

"I'll be in the X-ray department," he told her. "Call me as soon as Dr. Daniels arrives with his patient." And he turned abruptly and headed for the elevator.

Julia busied herself with the routine chores of the morning and had Millie Randall ready to take over for her should she be needed in the operating room. The ambulance was coming at ten to take Mrs. Myles, the diabetic, to Boston. There were medications to be administered, intravenous tubes to be looked after and the usual number of dressings to be changed. The minutes passed quickly.

Then Julia's phone rang, and the switchboard girl told her the emergency case had arrived. Julia asked the girl to notify Dave Farren in the X-ray room; then she put down the receiver and called Millie Randall.

The stout nurse hurried up to the desk. "Do you want me to take over now?" she asked.

Julia nodded. "I'll go downstairs. They're here. I may be some time."

Dr. Daniels was supervising the removal of the accident victim from a big station wagon when she arrived at the emergency entrance. The old doctor nodded to her brusquely and, indicating the inert patient on the blanket-covered stretcher, said: "It's pretty bad. He's under heavy sedation. Where's Dr. Farren?"

"He'll be right here," she promised.

Dave came as they spoke. And the two doctors discussed the situation in low voices by the stretcher in the emergency room.

At last Dave turned to Julia. "It means an open reduction. We have a transverse fracture of the fibula in one leg, and there's comminuted fracture in several areas of the other one. Get the O.R. ready."

A half-hour later she was assisting Dave as his scalpel exposed the sites of the complicated fractures. It was normally the task of an orthopedic specialist, but in this emergency well within the scope of Dave's ability.

Dr. Daniels bent over the patient at the opposite side of the table, his bushy eyebrows seeming more prominent than ever under the strong light. Julia kept instruments and clamps coming as Dave needed them. She'd worked with him as scrub nurse so many times she was aware of his needs almost before he spoke.

Dr. Daniels' voice rasped out, "He won't be doing any driving for six months or so."

Dave, still working grimly, murmured, "This will mean hospitalization in a cast for at least ten weeks."

"And all to save a few minutes' time," the veteran doctor snapped. "Wonder why they never learn?"

Dave was now near the end of the operation. He laughed shortly. "I've heard some funny stories about your heavy foot on the gas pedal, Doctor."

Dr. Daniels straightened slightly. "Malicious gossip! Nothing more! I've been driving for a half-century or longer, and I guess I know how to handle any kind of a car."

Julia was amused. She knew that Dave's accusation was true. The old doctor did drive his big Cadillac too fast. This small talk eased the tension at the operating table without distracting the participants from their work in any way.

Not many minutes after the incision was closed and the patient removed to a bed on Julia's own floor, Dave pulled off his mask and smiled at her. "Thanks for the good assistance, Nurse Lee."

Dr. Daniels hobbled over. "Glad I got you in time, Dr. Farren. Was afraid you might be off somewhere on calls and there'd be no one here to help me."

Dave smiled. "I was just sitting down to breakfast."

Old Dr. Daniels sighed. "Of course the accident had to happen just a mile from my place. Come to think of it, I haven't had anything to eat yet. We'd better both go down to the cafeteria."

Julia smiled knowingly at the circulating nurse as the two doctors walked away together. The comradeship between the veteran general practitioner and the young surgeon was obvious and touching. She hurriedly began to help clean up.

At the door to the scrub room Dr. Daniels paused to turn and ask: "What's the word on the ambulance for Mrs. Myles?"

"It's coming at ten," she told him.

"I'll be up to see her before then," the old man promised.

So the day began on a busy note. It continued that way until noon. Mrs. Bates, the gallstone patient, went down to the X-ray room for plates. Mrs. Martha Jones was discharged, and her husband came to take her home.

Julia went down for lunch at her usual time. She decided to eat in the cafeteria section and found a tray and selected an open beef sandwich and some light vegetables. Working so strenuously since early morning had given her an appetite. She'd just sat down with the meal when Dave appeared in the doorway. He saw her and went over and filled a tray for himself. Then he joined her at the corner table she'd selected.

Julia smiled at him. "It's usually proper for a gentleman to ask a young lady's permission before he joins her."

He gave her a slightly exasperated look. "I'd rather you didn't quote to me from the book of etiquette until you learn to manage your own behavior better."

"Meaning what?"

"The way you behaved last night!"

"I behaved?" She raised her eyebrows. "That vanishing act you did wasn't the sort of thing to give a girl confidence."

"You know why I left you," he said. "I was needed at the bar."

"I saw that," Julia observed dryly. "Edna must have been pining away there before you came."

"Mother thought the party wasn't gay enough," Dave protested. "It was her idea that Edna and I serve the drinks. She thought it made everything more personal and more fun as well."

"When you left me alone in that crowd, I didn't break down with laughter," Julia said tartly.

Dave sighed. "I know I neglected you for a while. But I left the bar as soon as I could. And I wasn't able to find you anywhere."

Julia smiled at him derisively. "You weren't really surprised?"

"It spoiled the night for me," he said.

Nevertheless, before the meal was over they had effected an uneasy reconciliation.

Julia had several phone calls from Bill

88

Dixon in the days that followed. He waited until she returned from work and called her at the house. Not wanting to complicate things any further, she put him off.

On Saturday evening he was persistent. "They're having a dance at the country club again," he said. "Why not let me take you?"

She didn't want to tell him directly that this would be the signal for all the local wagging tongues to go into action. She'd never attended a club dance with anyone but Dave. And if she arrived escorted by Bill Dixon, there was bound to be a lot of idle talk.

She said, "Let's wait until next week. A lot of the tourist crowd will be here for the July 4th weekend, and there'll be more doing. I'm tired tonight."

He reluctantly accepted her decision. "If you'd prefer that," he said. "We'll be having our own dance at the hotel next Saturday. How about then?"

"I'd like that," she agreed. It would be much better, since most of the guests there would be from out of town.

"I've got my boat ready," the young hotel owner went on. "Would you like to come out for a spin in it tomorrow?"

She laughed. "I hate to be so uncooperative. But I usually visit my Dad on Sundays. He's expecting me tomorrow."

Bill sounded like a disappointed boy. "Then that's out," he said.

"I have next Thursday afternoon off," she told him. "If you have any free time, I'd be glad to go then."

"I can usually manage a couple of hours," he said, his voice brighter. "I'll call you on Wednesday evening, and we can make plans."

Julia hung up the phone with a smile. Bill could be persistent, but he was nice about it. She knew that Dave would resent her seeing him. But there seemed no valid reason she shouldn't enjoy some of the summer fun with the likable Bill. After all, she wasn't engaged to Dave — at least not yet!

Dave always drove her up to her father's on Sunday afternoon and stayed while she prepared dinner. It had been a weekly ritual for some time, and she knew her father looked forward to the company and a meal he didn't have to cook for himself.

Sunday morning it began to rain, and by the time Dave came to pick her up there was a real downpour. She made a hasty run from the house to the convertible and slid in quickly beside the young doctor.

He smiled at her. "At least it will be good for the wells."

Julia slipped off her plastic rain hood and shook her head. "Down East folks have an excuse for any kind of weather."

Dave started the car, while the windshield wipers furiously strove to counteract the downpour. "It's true just the same. Some of the wells around here have been getting dangerously low."

"Spoken like a doctor and public health official," she teased him.

He kept his eyes on the road as they headed out of town. "Someone has to think of these things," he said. "Part of my job."

Julia remembered their other conversation about the town sewerage. "Have you had any word from the Dixons about the sewerage problem?"

Dave frowned. "Not yet. And I'd like to see something done as soon as possible."

"Have you discussed it with Bill?"

"Briefly," Dave said. "He wasn't too interested. Too busy supervising repairs at the hotel and getting that new boat of his in the water."

She studied the young doctor's stern profile. "You sound as if you think he won't be of much help."

"He won't," Dave said. "He told me to talk to Steve Malcomson when he comes."

"That's his manager?"

"Lawyer and manager," the young doctor said. "He takes care of the management of all the Dixon estate's affairs. He has the annual grant to the hospital in his hands, as well."

"I see," she said. "Then you've done business with him before?"

"On several occasions," Dave said. "He can be tough when he wants."

"And you think he'll be difficult now?"

"He's almost sure to be unless I can persuade him there's real danger. An epidemic in town could kill the hotel's business for a long while. If I can convince him of that, maybe he'll go along with the idea." Dave's tone became bitter. "If he thinks it's just for the benefit of the townspeople, he'll consider it a waste of money."

"You don't think the Dixons have much regard for the town?"

Dave took his eyes from the narrow, tree-lined road for a moment to glance at her. "No, I don't. What's your opinion?"

She shrugged. "I think you misjudge them. At least I think you're wrong about Bill. The night we talked, he seemed to have a real feeling for Wellsport."

92

"He's a natural born diplomat," Dave said. "You could depend on him to string you with that line. I'm impressed more by deeds than words."

She saw that the conversation was heading along dangerous lines and so let the subject drop. For the balance of the drive they talked about the weather and happenings at the hospital.

The rain eased somewhat as they pulled into her father's driveway. The heavy rain had turned the dirt road into a muddy mess, and Julia stepped carefully as she got out and made her way to the verandah. Her father was waiting for them in the doorway with a smile on his weather-beaten face.

"Wondered if you were going to come," he said.

Dave laughed. "I wouldn't think of missing one of Julia's home-cooked dinners."

They went inside, took off their wet coats and made themselves comfortable in the roomy kitchen. There was a good wood fire in the cookstove, and even on this late June afternoon the warmth was welcome in the face of the cold, driving rain. The temperature could drop surprisingly when wet, cloudy days came along. Dave stretched out comfortably on the old horsehair sofa that Julia remembered as part of the kitchen furnishings since she was a small girl.

Her father settled down at the table and was soon deeply engaged in reading the weekly paper which she always brought up with her. There was never much conversation until he'd digested all the news. Meanwhile Julia busied herself at the sink and stove preparing the chicken her father had waiting when she arrived.

It was a friendly, homey atmosphere, and Julia regarded these Sunday afternoons as among as the best times of her week. The rain had started to come down heavily again by the time she had the chicken dressed and in the oven. Dave rested with closed eyes and his hands behind his head, her father's jet black cat sprawled happily beside him in its own deep sleep.

As Julia closed the oven door, her father put down the paper and smiled at her. "I think that's more than enough news for now," he said.

She came over to the kitchen table and sat on the other side of it. "These lazy rainy days can be fun," she said.

He nodded. "All part of the pattern of nature." He glanced at the sleeping Dave. "Some rest won't do him any harm." Then to Julia, "Been a busy week at the hospital?"

"More so than usual," she admitted. And then she told him about some of the things that had happened. Her father was a good listener and had genuine interest in her doings.

"I suppose a lot of the summer people are showing up," he suggested.

She nodded. "The Dixons have been here quite awhile. The hotel opens the first of the week." She paused. "I had a talk with Bill Dixon. I didn't realize that you two had ever met."

Her father took off his glasses and carefully put them in their case. "Why, yes," he said. "He used to come up here quite a bit. That was years ago when he was just a boy."

"I don't remember," she said.

"Happened the years you were away at 4H Camp," Tom Lee said. "You remember you went for quite a few summers."

"That's when it was!" Julia said, understanding now. She'd gone to the youth camp several years in a row as a counsellor for some of the younger girls.

Her father took out his tobacco pouch and began filling his pipe. "He was a shy sort of lad, as I remember. But a good streak in him. He loved animals."

She laughed. "He mentioned a pet raccoon."

Tom Lee lit his pipe. "That was the last summer he came up here. I expect he was busy with college and other things later on." He paused to enjoy his pipe and then added, "We read some Thoreau together."

"He told me about that as well," she said.

Her father's shrewd eyes regarded her with interest. "You two must have gotten to know each other pretty well."

She smiled. "I suppose I questioned him when I found out he'd been up here. You can cover quite a lot of ground in a short conversation."

Tom Lee nodded. "Too bad about his wife. I heard he was badly broken up when she died. There's a child, isn't there?"

"A daughter. She's not at the hotel yet. But I understand she's coming later on in the summer."

"Well, I'm glad you two managed to meet," her father said.

"I'm not!" It was Dave who spoke out suddenly from the sofa. He swung his feet to the floor as he sat up and yawned. "Bill Dixon is all she wants to talk about."

"That's not true!" Julia laughed as she

96

got up to check on how her chicken was doing in the oven.

Dave sniffed the pleasant odor of the roasting bird and at the same time stroked the fur of the sleeping black cat. He addressed himself to Tom Lee.

"Julia thinks the Dixons are the royalty of Wellsport," he said. "And I think we can do without a ruling class."

Tom Lee laughed easily. "They've brought a lot of money to Wellsport with their hotel."

Dave raised his eyebrows. "That impresses you? I thought you were a devout believer in Thoreau's philosophy."

Her father said, "You mean such as, 'The man is richest whose pleasures are the cheapest'? I do think that is true."

"But you approve of the Dixons?"

Tom Lee shrugged. "They do provide a lot of work here. And in spite of their wealth, I've always found them rather pleasant people. Of course I don't know the young ones too well."

Julia joined the conversation. "You've met Bill."

Her father nodded. "Yes. And I've heard a lot about him from other people around here." He paused. "I suppose he's not all to blame. He's lived a difficult life."

"I'd call it pampered," Dave said derisively.

Her father shrugged. "Same thing. Perhaps he'd not be as he is if he hadn't lost his wife. But he does have one bad weakness."

Julia stared at him. "What sort of weakness?"

Tom Lee gave her a grave look. "One that could ruin him if he isn't careful. He's a compulsive gambler."

Chapter Six

Julia would not have been impressed by this statement if it had come from anyone else but her father. She knew how careful the cautious Tom Lee always was in making a pronouncement about anyone.

She said, "I've never heard anything like that."

Dave gave her a shrewd glance. "I have. Didn't pay much attention to it, since I hadn't any first-hand knowledge of his gambling myself." He looked at her father. "How did you find out?"

Tom Lee removed his pipe. "I have a friend who works at the race track in Scarborough Downs," he said. "From what he told me, young Dixon doesn't confine his betting to the pari-mutuel windows. He's been mixed up with some of the professional, big-time gamblers who hang around racetracks. Most of his betting has been with them."

Dave whistled softly. "I've heard about that crowd. A tough lot!"

Tom Lee nodded. "I wouldn't care to

welsh on a payment to them."

Julia found herself liking the picture less and less. She spoke defensively. "Maybe it's not as bad as you think. He might only have gone up there once or twice. You know how people talk about the Dixons! Everything is gossiped about and blown up out of all proportion."

Her father gave one of his quiet smiles. "I don't want to destroy any pleasant image you may have of the young man," he said. "But he's been there more than once. And this has gone on for several years."

"I heard about card games at the hotel for big stakes," Dave said. "The race track betting is new to me. But it all fits in."

Julia got up with a sigh. "That's how all these scandals start! Pretty soon you'll be believing it and enlarging on all the details." She moved to the stove. "The chicken is ready. Let's have dinner."

They sat around the big kitchen table and enjoyed the home-cooked meal. The talk changed to other things, and the dinner proved a completely enjoyable one. Dave teased Julia about her dressing and then, to prove he was joking about its being poor, requested a second helping. Afterward he even helped with the dishes while Tom Lee returned to finishing the weekly newspaper.

At last it was after nine and time to leave. Julia knew that her father liked to go to bed early and get up shortly after dawn. He'd followed this routine ever since he'd come to Maine to make his home. The rain still continued to come down heavily, and after they'd said goodbye to Tom Lee, they dodged out through the downpour and got in the convertible again.

"We should have a decent week after this," Dave said, starting the car. "There can't be much more rain left."

Sure enough, the next morning the weather reversed itself. The sky was blue and cloudless, and the warm July sun had already made itself felt by the time Julia arrived at the hospital. She went over the files with Laura Britt, and it occurred to her that her associate looked wan and worried. After giving Julia the keys, the other nurse lingered to make small talk about the weather. She also mentioned that her brother Willard had returned from Florida and that it would mean extra work for her while he remained in Wellsport.

Dave arrived at the usual time and, after seeing Mrs. Bates, decided that her gallstone operation should be scheduled for the next morning. He went along the rooms of his various patients with Julia at his side, making notes of changes in treatment and medication, where required.

Mrs. Molloy, the old woman with the broken hip, was now sitting up in a chair and was much brighter. Her wrinkled face creased in a smile when they entered her room.

"I feel fine this wonderful morning," she announced to them. "Why can't I go home, Doctor? I want to be sure my husband looks after my garden properly. He'll not do it if I'm away too long."

Dave Farren smiled. "I'll think about it," he promised. "We'll see how you make out this week."

"Another week!" the old woman exclaimed. "Surely you can do better than that?"

"I'll tell you when you'll be able to leave in another week," Dave corrected her. "So don't get any idea in your head that you'll be getting away from us next Monday."

"If you have to stay in this place, I should at least feel sick," the old woman grumbled in a joking way, winking at Julia as they left.

Jameson, the lobster fisherman with the slipped disc, was not nearly so mobile as he lay stretched out in his bed, rigid in the cast that Dave had prepared for him. The old man's ruddy face wore a look of exasperation.

"How much of this do I have to stand?" he wanted to know.

Dave asked, "How's the pain?"

"Just a whisper of it left," Jameson said. "I think you've cured me, Doctor."

"Not cured," Dave corrected him. "We've managed to control your pain by getting you in the cast. The cure will take time. But you're among the lucky ones. You won't have to go through an operation."

Jameson sighed. "Just what happened to me, Doc?"

"A disc between the bones of your spine slipped backward, probably because of the weakening of the fibrous ring holding it in place."

"Do people ever get well themselves from this kind of trouble?"

Dave nodded. "Yes. If they're not too bad. Of course there's always the chance it can recur again."

"How long do I have to stay in this straight jacket?" Jameson grinned.

"A fortnight," the young doctor told him, "providing you're a good patient." He smiled at Julia. "I'll warn you Miss Lee is my spy around here. And she'll report on how you behave."

"I'll be a good patient," Jameson promised. "I want to get back to work. This is my busy time of year."

They left the lobsterman, and Dave's round of calls was finished. They strolled back to the main desk, and Julia put down her notes, ready to transfer them to the various patients' charts and bring them up to date.

Dave smiled at her. "How long? That's all they want to know. There isn't one of them that doesn't get around to that question sooner or later. Probably Mrs. Bates will be asking the same thing before we even get to the O.R. tomorrow."

The rest of the day went by routinely. Tuesday was more hectic, with Julia dividing her time between the operating room and her duties as head nurse on the second floor. Mrs. Bates came through the operation nicely, with Dave doing the surgery and his father assisting.

Julia noticed the elder Dr. Farren in the scrub room afterwards and thought he looked extremely haggard. He was not an old man, but he seemed to lack both the enthusiasm and endurance of Dr. Daniels. And the veteran doctor must have been his senior by at least fifteen years.

On Wednesday they got the first of their

important summer patients. Millie Randall came up to Julia's desk, full of excitement. "Just guess who's downstairs?" she bubbled. "And he's going to be here on this floor!"

"One thing at a time." Julia smiled up at her. "Who is it?"

"Professor Disher," Millie said. "You know! The artist!"

Julia immediately had a mental picture of Professor William Disher. He had been a prominent figure in the summer community of Wellsport for as long as she could remember. He must be nearing seventy now, but he was a jaunty little man with a small merry face quite unlined with age, adorned by a tiny gray mustache and pointed beard. To complete his artistic appearance, he wore a dark blue beret, always at an angle, dark Bermuda shorts, a hard wing collar, black tie and tweed jacket.

He was liked by everyone in Wellsport because he was genial and had real talent. His paintings had been hung in fine galleries all over the world, and he had proven himself an outstanding interpreter of the Maine coastal region. His marine paintings were lifelike in color and detail and as much appreciated by the natives as by art connoisseurs who had never seen Maine.

He taught in a small college during the winter, but every summer saw him back at his studio in Wellsport.

The studio was a small building on the main street of Wellsport that had once been a notions store. Since notions stores had become unprofitable with the advent of a chain five and dime in Wellsport, the professor had picked up the one storey, two room building for a modest figure. The front room served as his studio and salesroom, and he lived in the back. The studio was a hodgepodge of paints, easels, brushes, paintings in frames, paintings on the floor leaning against one another, paintings piled on the counters, all presided over by the jaunty little figure in Bermudas.

The light from the windows was not right, as many other artists had pointed out to him. But Professor Disher was not in the least interested or bothered. Every day he painted, and often what he painted was extremely good. He made sales and he made friends, and people looked forward to his return every July.

"What's his trouble?" Julia wanted to know.

"The door was open in Dr. Farren's office, and I heard some of what they were saying," Millie Randall said. "I think it's his eyes."

"That doesn't surprise me," Julia observed. "He's been abusing them for years."

Dr. William Farren brought the patient upstairs about a half-hour later. He gave Julia one of his grave smiles as Professor Disher stood at his side, looking as sprightly as ever.

"You know Professor Disher," Dave's father said. "He has to have some treatment for his eyes. Will you please find a room for him so Dave and I can check on his condition during the next few days?"

Julia smiled at the old artist. "We have a small private room down at the end of the corridor with a nice view of the cove."

The artist nodded. "Fine. Not that I'll be able to see it for a while. But it will give me something to look forward to."

Julia sent him down to the room in the charge of an excited Millie Randall. When they were alone, Dr. William Farren turned to her and said: "Cataracts. He'll have to have an operation. I want Dave's confirming opinion. But I have no doubt."

"You'll want him to have bed rest for a few days, then," Julia said.

The bald man sighed. "Yes. I want him

to have a thorough medical and dental check-up. We want to be sure his chest is clear; coughing during surgery or afterward can have a very unfavorable effect on the outcome of the operation. Bad teeth may be his source of infection and give us trouble later as well."

"You'll want a check on whether or not he shows any signs of diabetes, won't you, Doctor?"

"The urine must be examined carefully for sugar," Dr. William Farren agreed. He gave her a pleased look. "You're alert to symptoms, young lady, since you know that diabetes is often a cause of cataract formation. You trained in Boston, didn't you?"

She nodded. "Yes. I happened to have quite a few patients who'd undergone eye surgery."

"It's encouraging to find a young nurse so interested in her profession and apparently so well trained," he said. "I'll have Dave come by and see the professor as soon as possible." With that, he took the elevator downstairs.

Millie came back to the desk shortly with a despairing smile. "You'd better drop by and see the professor. I've gotten him in bed, but he's done nothing but ply me with questions, mostly ones I can't answer."

"I'll see him after lunch," Julia promised.

At that time she discovered Millie had been right. The professor was full of questions. He sat propped up against the pillows like a bright gnome, the twinkle in his eyes belying the fact that his vision was dangerously clouded.

"Found I couldn't work any more," the man with the beard confided in her. "When that happened, there was nothing else to do but come here."

"You shouldn't have waited," Julia said. "There's no need to these days."

He sighed. "I'd like to take advantage of part of the summer. Do you think I'll get over the operation in time to do some painting?"

"I think so," she said. "You should be able to work again in six weeks."

His face became gloomy. "Do I have to stay in bed that long?"

Julia laughed. "No. You'll be back in your studio by then. You'll only have to stay in bed about a week."

Professor Disher brightened. "You make it sound better. I've been here thinking all kinds of things. Will I need a private nurse?"

"It would be better," she advised, "for a few days, while your eyes are still bandaged."

The old artist looked at her shyly. "Will it hurt?"

"The post-operative period is not painful," she told him.

"I'm not sorry to hear that," he said. "I suppose I'll have always to wear glasses."

She nodded. "The glasses are ground and curved to take over the function of your own damaged natural lens."

Professor Disher sighed. "I guess I'm a vain old man. But I always prided myself on my good eyesight. Never wanted to wear glasses." He gave her a sudden look as if a new idea had hit him. "Could I wear contact lenses?"

"I've known of them being worn when only one eye was operated on," she recalled. "I think you should be able to. Talk to Dr. Farren about it." And she went back to her desk, leaving the little man in a happier state of mind.

She and Dave Farren went for a drive on Wednesday night. She deliberately refrained from revealing her plan to see Bill Dixon on Thursday, and luckily Dave didn't think to ask her what she was doing on her afternoon off.

They stopped at one of the better roadside restaurants and had lunch. The place was filled, and Dave looked around at the

110

crowd of tourists and frowned.

"The flood is on us," he said. "And I haven't had a word from the mayor or Dixon's attorney."

Julia studied his determined young face across the table. "Do you think they're deliberately ignoring your letters?"

He twisted a matchbook in his fingers in an impatient gesture. "It looks like it," he said.

"What will you do if they don't get in touch with you?"

"I'll give them until the end of the week," Dave declared. "After that I'm making a fight of it. And I'll use whatever tactics I have to."

Julia was impressed by his quiet sincerity. "You really think there is danger, don't you?"

He showed slight anger. "With the cove contaminated as it will be when another thousand or so tourists hit town, I know that the odds are we'll have trouble. I worried all last year and this year. If this place is an example, we're going to have more visitors than ever."

"What could happen?"

Dave sighed. "So many things, and all of them unpleasant, that I'd rather not think about them. And when trouble comes, don't doubt that they'll find some way to make it look as if Dad and I have neglected our duty."

She raised her eyebrows. "How could they possibly do that?"

"We're responsible for the health situation here, public and private," Dave said tersely. "Dad is head of the hospital, and I have the largest local practice. Dr. Daniels depends on us to take the lead in everything; he's actually as good as retired."

"You said there wasn't time to do much this year," she reminded him.

"Some precautions can be taken," he said. "And a beginning could be made getting a new sewerage disposal plant for the town. But not the way the Council and the Dixon crowd are evading the threat."

Julia was convinced of the young doctor's sincerity. But she could not believe that the town officials and the Dixons would deliberately do anything to jeopardize people's health or hurt their business. There must be two sides to the question. It was another thing she hoped to find out more about from Bill Dixon when she saw him the following afternoon.

Chapter Seven

Thursday was fine and warm. After the heavy rainstorm that had lasted all through Sunday, the weather seemed to have taken a turn for the better. Julia spent a busy morning at the hospital and was glad when lunch time arrived.

Just before she left, there was a call from Dr. Daniels. The veteran doctor had not been around the hospital for several days. She judged that he must have a new patient to be admitted, and this proved correct.

"That you, Miss Lee?" he asked in his familiar rasping tone.

"Yes, Dr. Daniels," she said. "Can I help you?"

"You can," he said bluntly. "I need a bed for a special patient. I've talked with Dr. Farren, and he said I'd better call you directly. Colonel Morris is at the Manorview for the summer again. And he's having some trouble."

Julia recognized Colonel Morris' name. He was a retired army officer who now was president of a large manufacturing firm. He was a tall, white-haired man with a hawk-like face. She remembered waiting on him at the hotel years back, and he'd seemed elderly to her then.

"We have several nice private rooms available," she said. "I assume he'd like one of the larger, airier ones?"

"The best," Dr. Daniels said in his terse way. "He'll be coming in after two."

"I won't be here then," Julia explained. "This is my afternoon off. But I'll see that Nurse Randall is informed. She'll see that he's well taken care of."

"I will depend on that," the old doctor said. "The colonel is an old friend of mine as well as my patient. I suspect he is suffering from Meniere's Disease. But we will keep him for a few days for tests."

As soon as she hung up, Julia gave all the details to Millie Randall. The stout girl looked unhappy as she listened.

"I know him by sight," she said. "I've heard he's one of the richest men in the country. And he's so austere. I'm frightened of him. I wish you were going to be here instead of me."

"Get Jane Freeman to help you," Julia suggested.

Millie tossed her head. "She's no help!

114

All she does is run around and wring her hands when things get mixed up. I'll manage on my own somehow." Then, considering: "What kind of a disease did you say he had?"

"Meniere's Disease," Julia told her. "It's a condition where there's an acute disturbance of the structure of the internal ear. It's named after a French doctor. The chief symptoms are deafness, dizziness, and sometimes nausea. Usually the attacks come and go."

"Well, let's hope he's not feeling too badly when he arrives," Millie Randall said. "He'll probably be hard enough to cater to when he's feeling well."

Julia had lunch in the cafeteria, but there was no sign of Dave. She had heard him mention going to Portland. Since he'd had no operations scheduled for that morning, she supposed that was where he'd gone.

When she left the hospital she decided to walk to the center of the town and pick up a few things in the big drugstore opposite the small square. She needed a new bathing cap, and since there was a chance she might want to swim during the afternoon, she decided to get it at once. There were also a few other items such as a lipstick and stockings. The drugstore was stocked with so many sundries that most people thought of it as a small department store rather than merely a pharmacy.

She pushed her way through the swinging glass doors and went directly to the counter that featured bathing suits and caps. She spent a few minutes before she found a white one that suited her. As she prepared to move to the cosmetics counter, she saw two familiar figures coming across the store toward her: Mrs. Emily Farren and Edna Dixon!

Dave's mother was wearing a stylish print dress and wide straw hat, and Edna had on blue slacks and pale blue turtle neck sweater to match. Both women were talking and seemed to be thoroughly enjoying their shopping tour. Emily Farren spotted Julia at almost the same instant she recognized the older woman. The reaction on the part of Dave's mother was startling. The happy smile she'd been wearing faded, and her expression became coldly blank. Deliberately she pretended not to see Julia and headed the tall girl at her side to the counter opposite. It was a deliberate snub!

Julia felt her cheeks burn, but she was actually more amused than angered. Dismissing the incident as well as she could, she hurried over to the cosmetics counter and made her other purchases. She was on her way to the cashier's desk when she heard Edna Dixon call out behind her.

"Julia Lee!" the blonde girl said. "I didn't expect to see you here at this time of day. Have they closed the hospital?"

Julia smiled as she turned to her. "I have this afternoon off."

"Isn't that nice?" Edna said condescendingly. "I think it's right working people should take more time off."

"I really don't worry about it," Julia replied coolly, "just as long as I know I'm being useful."

It was the tall girl's turn to color. She managed a smile. "Yes, I suppose that is important."

Emily Farren came up and joined them, giving Julia a sour smile. "Are you enjoying the summer?" she asked.

Julia said, "I've been having a wonderful time, even on Sunday when it was so wet. Dave and I drove up to my Dad's little farm, and I cooked a chicken for us all in the old-fashioned stove. It was fun!"

Edna's nose tilted a full notch higher, and Mrs. Emily Farren looked completely shaken as her mouth opened slightly. But for once she could find no cutting reply. Satisfied that she'd handled the meeting as well as possible, Julia gave them a parting smile and hurried on to the cashier.

She wore a white sports dress with a pleated skirt and round neck. She also had her bathing suit and some sun tan lotion and glasses in a beach bag which she was taking with her. Bill had called promptly at two o'clock and was now on his way to pick her up.

Sarah Thomas sat on the verandah with her and gave her an admiring appraisal. "You look nice in white," the matronly woman said. "Dark people always do."

"I like it for summer wear," Julia said.

"You'll knock that Bill Dixon's eye out," Sarah predicted. "You'll be the prettiest girl around the hotel. Most of those moneyed women have no looks at all."

Julia stood up as she saw Bill's car come down the hill. "Here he is now," she said.

Sarah Thomas made a quick run to the door. "I mustn't let him see me in this old dress," she said, "or he'll think you're living with a gypsy." She went inside and out of sight.

Julia laughed and then went on out to the sidewalk as Bill parked. She said, "You're very punctual."

He smiled as she got into the car beside

him. "I don't deserve credit for that. It's just that I'm anxious to spend as long as possible in the new boat." He eyed her beach bag. "I hope you brought along a bathing suit."

"I did," she said. "I thought I might be able to go in the water."

"Not in the ocean," he said, starting the car and turning it around to go back to the hotel. "It's too cold, and in the cove it's too crowded with the regular tourists from town. We'll take a dip in the hotel pool when we get back from our boat trip."

"Sounds like fun," she said. She thought Bill looked very athletic and handsome in white Bermuda shorts and a dark blue sports shirt. And since he'd mentioned the cove and the crowded conditions there, she thought it might be a good time to say something about the sewerage problem.

She said, "I don't think I'd like swimming in the cove. It is crowded, as you say. And I always have the feeling the water can't be too clean."

"It isn't," Bill agreed at once. "The town sewerage flows into part of the area, and according to your friend Dave Farren the water is contaminated to the danger point."

"Do you think it is, too?"

He shrugged, keeping his eyes on the road. "I wouldn't know. I'd never think of swimming in the cove, anyhow, so I'm not too interested."

She persisted, "But so many people do swim there. It could cause illness on a large scale if it got bad enough."

Bill shot her a reproving glance. "Don't you start our afternoon off with a lot of scary nonsense. Leave that to Dr. Dave. This is our day for fun."

She saw there was no use trying to talk about it further. It would only annoy him.

Bill had his own parking lot with a reserved sign near the main entrance to the big yellow and white Manorview House. The lovely grounds were enhanced by sunlight, and Julia was impressed by the beauty of the place.

She stood for a moment taking it all in. "No wonder people like to come here," she said at last.

Bill laughed and, taking her by the arm led her around the building to the rear lawn. "We work hard to make it fun for our guests," he said. "And it isn't as easy as it seems."

"I have an idea," she said, keeping in step with him. "Don't forget I was one of your employees once, if just a lowly one."

He smiled down at her. "We were lucky to have you here," he said. And then, as they came around the building and could see the big swimming pool: "This is new since your time here."

She nodded. "It looks marvelous." She took in the rows of deck chairs with colored umbrellas for those who wanted shelter from the sun. At one end of the sparkling blue pool there were two diving boards, one high and a lower one for less experienced swimmers.

"We'll try this on our way back," he assured her.

They strolled down a path that led to the water. The hotel had a beach and private wharf here, although the beach was little used now that the pool had been built. The wharf, however, was the scene of a good deal of activity, and Julia saw that there were quite a number of different-sized boats moored there.

On the way down the hill, they passed the hotel's nine hole golf course on the right. This was one place she remembered from the days when she'd been a waitress. On certain afternoons she'd had to work at the canteen near the course.

The wharf was larger than it looked from a distance, and when they got there Bill led her to where an unusually long, sleek cabin cruiser was moored. He helped her from the wharf down into the big white craft, and his smile showed that he was enjoying the awe with which she took it in.

"It's forty-three feet long," he told her. "Has two V8 water-cooled engines for two hundred and twenty-five horsepower and a comfortable layout for eight people."

"I've never seen anything so nice," she exclaimed.

He made his way toward the wheel-house. "Wait until you've seen her in action," he said proudly.

Just then a man wearing a yachting cap came to the side of the dock and peered over. "Ahoy, Bill!" he said jovially. He was dark, close to middle age and dressed in dark trousers and shirt.

Bill Dixon left the wheel and went over to him. "Just going out for a spin," he told the man on the dock.

"Good day for it," said the man. And then, "We're going to have a return game tonight, in my room. Can we count you in?"

Bill laughed. "I wouldn't miss it. Give me a chance to get even."

"See you later then." The man on the dock waved and moved out of sight.

Bill passed her on his way back to the wheel. "One of our guests," he said. "The kind who comes down to play cards every night."

Julia said nothing. But the interchange had convinced her that the story her father had told about Bill's gambling had some basis of truth. The racing season at Scarborough Downs would be starting in another week, and she was willing to bet he'd be spending a lot of his time there.

The motors started with a surprising volume of noise. One of the workers on the wharf cast off the line for Bill, and in a moment they were heading out across the blue water. The boat quickly picked up speed and swayed gently as a fine spray of water was left in its wake. Bracing herself slightly, she stared back at the rapidly receding wharf and the town of Wellsport to the right. The cove was filled with small craft, and now that they were in open water they passed many other boats, some of them slim sailboats with colorful striped sails.

Bill shouted to her, "Why be so aloof? Come up here by me."

In the excitement of the moment she forgot about her disappointment in him. She stood close to him and brushed back a strand of hair from her face. "The wind is cooler out here," she said.

"Always is," he agreed. And then, with a gesture toward the vast horizon of blue water in front of them, "The only uncrowded highway left."

"If boating stays as popular as it is, there won't even be this," Julia observed.

"It's more crowded than it was a few years ago," he said. "But Maine still offers lots of water space."

Now he guided the boat parallel to the coast and showed her the many estates built overlooking the ocean. There was also a new motel, situated dramatically at the top of a sheer cliff so the breakers dashed against the rocks hundreds of feet below. There was a spouting cavern where the pressure of the incoming tide blew water from the rock wall in an impressive fountain-like display. Farther on there was a small island where it was rumored, Bill said, Captain Kidd had once buried treasure. But no one had ever found more than a few gold coins and some rusty iron padlocks. He seemed to know all the fascinating lore of the coast, and she found his stories as dramatic as any of the ones her father had told her.

She smiled at him. "You make it all seem so real."

They cruised back in a more leisurely manner, and Bill talked of his experiences in boating and how he'd come to buy this particular craft. Julia listened, aware that he was enjoying one of his few enthusiasms.

She said, "Does Edna come out with you often?"

His face showed distaste. "Edna doesn't like the water. The slightest swell, and she's seasick. Anyhow, we don't get on too well."

This was news to Julia, although she wasn't surprised.

Finally they headed back to the wharf again. Julia was reluctant to have the pleasant cruise come to an end, but since they both wanted a dip in the pool, it was time to come in.

"We'll do it again soon," Bill promised.

She laughed. "Don't forget that I spend most of my afternoons in a hot hospital ward."

"Surely you'll have other days off," he said, staring at her.

"I'll try when your Karen gets here," she told him, "providing you aren't too busy at Scarborough Downs."

"I'll find the free time," he said hastily, and then busied himself bringing the big pleasure craft safely in to the dock. They went up to the hotel, changed to their bathing suits and spent more than an hour in and around the pool. Aside from a few kiddies, the lifeguard, and some of the younger couples, the pool was quite deserted in the late afternoon.

When they had tired themselves out, they stretched side by side on the comfortable deck chairs to sop up some of the remaining afternoon sun. Bill raised himself on an elbow and studied Julia. "You belong here," he said. "You're right for this place."

She smiled. "Thank you. But I'm afraid the rates are beyond my purse."

"I don't mean as a guest," he said. "I'd like you here at my side as my wife."

Julia tried to cover her confusion with a light, incredulous laugh. "That's a flattering approach. I'm sure all the girls you've had here have been impressed."

Bill showed hurt. "That's not a stock speech. I said it just for you." His face clouded. "In fact, I never expected to say anything like that again."

She was genuinely touched. "Thank you," she told him quietly. "Let's just put it down to a lovely day and good company. It's really been very nice."

His eyes met hers. "Don't say that no one ever proposed to you."

"I won't," she promised. "I'll remember it through the years," she went on with a mocking note of laughter in her voice. "I'll tell my grandchildren, if any, about it."

He came out of his temporary gloom with a shrug and a laugh. "Well, if you prefer to think it was funny, then it was funny!"

She sat up. "It wasn't funny! But it's hardly the time or the place."

Bill showed interest. "Can you suggest a time and place?"

"I'll give it my closest consideration," she promised with a smile. "Now I'm beginning to feel cold, and I think I'd better change."

They changed back into their clothes, and he drove her home. They were both in a relaxed, happy mood. And when she said goodbye to him, it marked the end of one of the most enjoyable afternoons she'd ever known.

Next morning Dave came to the hospital early to examine Professor Disher. He also made the rounds of his other patients, and Julia thought he was in a strangely subdued humor. She wondered how he'd made out in Portland the previous day and decided to ask him if they met at lunch.

He came to the desk with her as they finished their rounds and said, "I'm going to schedule the professor's cataract operation for Monday, at least his first one. I've explained that it's standard practice to do just one eye at a time and wait four to six months before doing the next one."

She smiled. "Just so long as he knows he'll have enough sight to paint with at the end of the first operation."

Dave nodded. "I assured him that he would. And he seems reconciled. At first he insisted I do both eyes at once. Wanted to get it over with." And then with a change of tone he asked casually, "Will you be having lunch at the usual time?"

"I'll be down shortly after twelve," she said.

"I'll see you then," he told her. And he went downstairs.

Millie Randall approached her with a worried expression. "I wish Dr. Daniels would get here. That Colonel Morris has been sick again."

"Is he over it now?"

"He says he's feeling better," the stout nurse said. "But I doubt it will last long. He's been having these spells ever since he came in."

"Perhaps I'd better call Dr. Daniels," Julia decided.

The old doctor listened to her patiently and then said, "I'll be over right away. I thought he was resting quietly. I've been considering putting him on a diet, or we may have to send him to Boston for surgery of the inner ear."

"Is there anything immediate we can do to ease his condition?" Julia asked.

"I'll see when I get there." Dr. Daniels sighed. "I'll read up on some of your new-fangled wonder drugs. I think dramamine and bonamine have been found of some value in controlling the symptoms."

After the phone conversation, Julia went in to see the old colonel. She found him resting quietly in the shadowed room, his eyes closed. Since he seemed to be asleep, she decided not to wake him. It was the first time she'd had a good look at him since he'd been admitted, and she was shocked to notice how much he'd aged and how thin he was compared to the man she recalled from her days as a waitress at the hotel. This wan, emaciated figure in the bed looked little like the stately retired soldier she'd seen striding across the golf course.

She had Millie take over and went down to the cafeteria. Dave was already there in one of the booths, and he rose and beckoned to her. She joined him, and they ordered. Then he looked at her across the table.

"About yesterday —" he said.

"Yes?" she inquired lightly.

"I suppose you thought it funny I went off to Portland so suddenly."

She smiled. "I didn't think too much about it. I assumed there was a good reason."

"There was," he said. "We know now who was responsible for the thefts of drugs on your floor."

Chapter Eight

Julia showed surprise. "I hadn't heard anything for quite a while. I thought the thefts had ended."

"They didn't." Dave shook his head. "They continued on a small scale even after the locks were changed."

She frowned. "Then that could only mean —" Her voice trailed off.

Dave completed the sentence for her. "It meant that someone in charge of the cabinet was taking the drugs. It more or less narrowed it to Grace Perkins, Laura Britt and you."

"And now you know who the guilty party is."

Dave nodded. "Dad questioned her yesterday. He already had more than a suspicion who it might be. She confessed. Laura Britt took the drugs."

"But why?"

"For her brother. He's a drug addict. He came here for the Scarborough Downs racing season as usual. She discovered his condition and was afraid of what he might do if he didn't have his supply of narcotics. So she began stealing for him."

"That's awful." Julia sighed. "She's such a wonderful person. What is your father going to do about it?"

"He's going to give her another chance," Dave said. "You're the only one who'll know anything about it, besides him and me and the authorities. Her brother got in a scrape in Portland and is in jail now. As I understand it, they're planning to send him to Lexington, Kentucky to take the cure."

"So he won't be bothering Laura any more."

"We hope not, and we've warned her to let us know if he does try anything when he gets out." The young doctor paused and shrugged. "I'm not too hopeful about the results of his cure. But just as long as he doesn't come back here to torment her —"

"She's a fine nurse," Julia said. "I'm glad your father gave her another chance."

"Dad always tries to be fair," Dave said.

"I know," she agreed.

"By the way," Dave said too casually, "this brother of Laura Britt's was one of a group that Bill Dixon hangs around with at Scarborough Downs."

Julia looked shocked. "You're not suggesting that he's been mixed up in anything like that."

Dave sipped his coffee. "No. But I'm trying to let you know the kind of company his gambling introduces him to."

She sighed. "It's too bad."

Dave gave her a smile. "Did you have a nice time on his boat yesterday?"

She looked at him with wry amusement. "So you did hear about it?"

"I walked right into it," he said. "I wanted to get in touch with Bill when I came back, and the girl in his office said he was out in his new boat with Miss Lee." He grinned across the table at her. "I didn't even ask."

"As long as you know," she said, "I might as well confess we had a wonderful time."

Dave played it cool. "Why not? That's a prize boat."

She felt any further discussion of the incident might lead to trouble. She glanced at her wristwatch.

"I must get back to my floor," she said. "It's getting late."

"I'm due up there as well," he said. "Dr. Daniels is coming in and wants me to look at a patient with him."

She raised her eyebrows. "Colonel Morris?"

"Right the first time," he said. "Dr. Daniels doesn't often indulge in a consultation. I gather the colonel must be pretty ill."

"He looks very bad," Julia agreed. "I stopped by his room before lunch. I'd say he's in critical shape."

Dave showed special interest in her description of the patient. He said, "Dr. Daniels has put it down as Meniere's Disease. But I don't think he's certain."

"All I can say is that Colonel Morris has failed terribly. I hardly recognized him."

Dave looked doubtful. "It sounds too drastic a change to put it down to Meniere's. I have an idea it might be something else, something that would show approximately the same symptoms."

"Such as?"

"It could be several things."

She eyed him closely. "But you have a hunch about what you should look for?"

"Yes," he admitted. "I wouldn't be surprised if we found there's a brain tumor."

"Of course!" she exclaimed. "I should have thought of that myself."

"It's only a rash guess," he cautioned her. "I haven't even seen the patient."

"I think it's a good one," Julia said. "At any rate, you'll soon know. Dr. Daniels promised to come in early. He's probably waiting for you now."

They went up to the second floor and found the veteran doctor in impatient conversation with Millie Randall, who was defensively pretending to be occupied with the charts spread out before her on the desk. They both turned their heads as the elevator door opened and Julia and Dr. Dave Farren emerged. Seeing them, Millie Randall beamed with relief, while Dr. Daniels scowled in their direction.

He pointed to the wall clock. "You're late. I've been waiting here ten minutes."

Dave smiled at the old man. "Actually, I'm five minutes early," he said. "I wasn't to be here until a quarter past."

Dr. Daniel's grouchy manner remained unchanged. "So I came early," he said. "Let's not quibble while a sick patient is waiting. Come along." And he led the way, hobbling quickly down the corridor. Dave flashed Julia a smile and followed him.

Millie groaned. "Did I ever get a calling-down for nothing! I'm glad you came when you did. That old Daniels has been taking all his spite out on me."

"I can understand that; he's worried," Julia said, sitting beside her. "I wouldn't be surprised if the patient died."

"Not on this shift, I hope," Millie Randall said, and got up.

Julia was left alone at the desk. Several phone calls came in, and she took them. At the same time she was checking on her card file. While she worked, the two doctors came slowly up the corridor in serious conversation. They stopped within earshot of her, and she couldn't help overhearing what they said.

Dr. Daniels' bass rumble was clearly audible as he told Dave, "I'm convinced now it isn't Meniere's Disease."

"I doubted it from the first," Dave agreed. "My guess is a brain tumor."

There was a short silence. "I'm afraid you may be right," Dr. Daniels at last admitted reluctantly. "The symptoms are the same: headache, vomiting, and disturbed balance and vision."

"So now we must look further," Dave said.

"There'll have to be other tests," the old doctor agreed wearily. "I don't like it, at the colonel's age. I don't know how he'd stand up under a brain operation, and if it's malignant there's not much point."

"If it should happen to be a meninglioma on the covering of the brain or a neuro-fibroma interfering with the nerves and it wasn't malignant, the operation wouldn't be too difficult for the patient and there'd be a first class chance of recovery," Dave pointed out, obviously trying to lift the veteran doctor's spirits.

Dr. Daniels sounded more hopeful as he replied, "That's true. Or it could be a pituitary tumor, and we might send him to Boston and have it treated by X-ray without any operation."

"If it's a brain tumor it means Boston anyway," Dave said. "Does he have any family here?"

"His wife," Dr. Daniels said. "They've been spending the summer at the Manorview for years. This is going to be a great shock to her, and she's rather frail." He paused. "Of course if it is a glioma and the tumor has developed within the brain itself, the chances are it's malignant and, no matter what we do, it'll only be a matter of time."

"It's too bad," Dave said. "You've been close friends."

"I'm very fond of the colonel," the old doctor agreed heavily. "The first move should be to confirm the location of the tumor."

"We can try plain X-rays here," Dave suggested, "and then an injection of radioactive substance. If we don't come up with anything, we may as well get him to Boston as quickly as possible."

Dr. Daniels nodded and came across to Julia. "Miss Lee, we'll be wanting the colonel to have certain tests. I'll send the X-ray technician up shortly. Will you please stand by to help in any way you can?"

Julia got up. "Of course. Just let me know what you need."

Within a half-hour the X-rays were taken and Dave proceeded with the other tests.

When Julia left the hospital there still had been no definite word about the plates or the other tests. She smiled at Laura Britt, who'd taken over and now sat in her chair. "I may phone in later. I'm curious to know what their diagnosis will be."

The pale woman nodded. "I'll phone you at the house if I hear anything."

"Thanks," Julia said. "It's not often I find myself so interested in a patient. But the colonel is different."

"I know." Laura Britt smiled sadly. "He's a part of the town. If anything happens, he'll be missed in Wellsport."

It was another fine afternoon. Julia walked to her boarding place, enjoying the air. She was part way up the stairs when

Sarah Thomas bustled out from the kitchen and called to her from the lower landing.

"There was a phone message from the hospital," Sarah said. "Dr. Dave Farren. He said he'd like you to call there as soon as you came in."

"Oh, thank you!" Julia smiled as she hurried back down.

She quickly put the call through to the hospital, and in a moment Dave's crisp young voice came over the line. "Laura Britt told me you were anxious to hear about the colonel. We've come up with something."

"I'm glad," she said. "What's the verdict?"

"The X-rays aren't conclusive," Dave said. "But the radioactive solution did help us locate the growth. I'm afraid it's involved in the brain tissue directly, a malignant glioma. We're rushing him to Boston by ambulance at once. I'm sending a special nurse with him."

"What about his wife?" she asked.

"She's going to ride up in the ambulance as well," Dave said. "There's no easy way for her, but I feel it's better she be close to him."

"We'll miss him striding through the town," Julia commented.

"The chances of his being here again are small," Dave said, "but we can still hope. Dr. Daniels is driving up to Boston tomorrow to talk with the doctors at the Lahey Clinic who will be handling the case."

"So we'll know more when he gets back," she said.

Then Dave sprang a bombshell. "By the way," he said quietly, "in all this excitement I forgot to tell you Edna Dixon is having an affair to repay Mother for her party. It's being held at the country club. She's having it tonight, and we're invited."

Julia didn't want to go. She hesitated, then said, "This is short notice."

"Don't tell me your social calendar is that full," he said. "We need only stay a little while. We can go somewhere else later."

"I'd rather not, Dave," she said.

"It would make it easier for me if you came." His voice held a quiet urgency. "I'll be tied up tomorrow night. I promised to go to a medical meeting in Portland. So I won't see you until we go up to your father's place on Sunday."

Julia sighed. "All right. I'll go. But I warn you in advance I won't like it."

His voice was plaintive. "If you feel that

way before you even arrive there, you're bound to be miserable. It might be fun. They're having a beachcomber night. So wear some old clothes. I'll pick you up about nine."

The news that it was to be a costume party brought on a new crisis. She had to decide what to wear. Sarah Thomas entered into the spirit of the thing and plagued Julia with wild suggestions and hand-me-downs that she was convinced would be suitable for any character Julia wanted to dress like, from a mermaid to a pirate girl.

After much discussion, she decided to go as a South Sea Island maiden. She had a sarong type brilliantly colored print dress. By adapting the top of it to bare her shoulders, she made it suitable. About the only other things she needed were sandals and a flower for her hair. Both of these were available.

By five minutes to nine Julia stood in front of Sarah Thomas for final approval. She'd applied a coating of a sun tan lotion that stained her skin slightly and the matronly woman had come out proudly bearing a pair of ivory white earrings.

"Just the thing you need, dear," she said, insisting that Julia put them on.

"Do I really look all right?" Julia asked the buxom woman.

"Just like you stepped out of one of them travel advertisements," Sarah Thomas replied.

Dave seemed just as enthusiastic when he arrived. He said, "You're the South Seas type. I didn't realize it before."

Julia gave a hopeless smile. "You two are just getting me ready for a big let-down. I'll probably be the worst dressed person at the party."

Dave grinned and indicated his ragged dungarees, black and yellow striped sweater and faded yachting cap. "I'm in line for that prize," he told her.

As they left the car at the club, she was glad to note they'd been parked some distance from the nearest of the many other cars that were there. Coming closer to the club building, they could plainly hear the orchestra. Dancing had already started.

Edna Dixon was standing at the entrance when they came in. She was wearing a white yachting outfit that suited her but was not like any beachcomber's dress that Julia could imagine.

She gave them a friendly smile of welcome. "You both look wonderful," she cried. And then, with a gesture toward herself, "I'm a rich beachcomber, so the dress is okay."

Another party arrived, and Julia was delighted that Edna had to give her attention to greeting them. She escaped with Dave, and they headed upstairs to the ballroom. The place was filled with people in every sort of costume. Many of the summer people had borrowed clothing from the lobster fishermen and had come costumed as Maine seaside characters. The local people, on the other hand were more imaginative. Their ranks included sailors, pirates, dancing girls and, proving Sarah Thomas had had the right idea, even mermaids! Julia soon felt at ease in her outfit.

She was thankful that so far she'd not encountered Emily Farren. When the dancing stopped for an intermission and the excited, chattering crowd spread out a bit, many going downstairs for additional refreshments, she got her first glimpse of the elder woman. She was sitting in the corner of the room most distant from the orchestra with her husband and two other older couples. None of them was in costume, the women wearing formal evening gowns, the husbands in white summer dinner jackets. Emily Farren did not seem to be enjoying herself too much, and Julia had an idea Edna's idea of a party did not win her full approval.

Dave had gone downstairs to get them cold drinks. Now he returned and gave her one. He said, "It's quite an affair. I didn't give Edna credit for so much imagination."

Julia smiled. "She is full of surprises and hidden qualities."

He eyed her sharply. "Are you trying to sell her to me?"

"Not at all," she said. "I'm just stating a fact."

"From what Dad told me when I saw him below," Dave said, "Mother isn't as pleased with this party as everybody else seems to be. And it's in her honor."

"I don't think she likes the costumes," Julia suggested sipping her drink and allowing her eyes to stray in the direction of Mrs. Farren again.

Dave followed her glance and stared at his mother. "She's in a mood. I can tell even at this distance."

"Hello, Dave!" a boisterous voice called out, and a stout young man dressed in a lobsterman's sweater, heavy trousers and cap strode over to them. He had a round, jolly face and double chins.

"Hello, Steve," the young doctor said. And, turning to Julia, "This is Julia Lee

144

from the Dixon Memorial Hospital. Meet Steve Malcomson, the man responsible for your weekly pay check."

Steve Malcomson laughed loudly and bowed to Julia. "Nice to meet you, Miss Lee. And don't pay any attention to Dave. He's always talking nonsense."

Dave's square young features took on a grim look. "That seems to be the general opinion."

"You're to blame!" the Dixons' lawyer said, poking a finger playfully in Dave's ribs. "Trying to scare Bill Dixon and his sister with all this talk of polluted water!"

Chapter Nine

Dave looked so annoyed that Julia was afraid for a moment he might be going to punch the boisterous young lawyer. Instead he clenched his fists at his side and answered in a controlled voice, "I merely placed some unpleasant facts before them."

"I've read the whole thing," Steve Malcomson said. "Not worth getting bothered about, I can tell you that. It's just what I said — a scare report!"

Julia glanced around at the groups near them, talking gaily with glasses in hand, a typical country club gathering. It was the most unlikely setting for this argument between the two men.

Dave said, "You think there's nothing to worry about."

"That puts it in a nutshell." Malcomson laughed. "Couldn't do it better myself, Miss Lee!" He turned and included her in the conversation.

"Polluted water could cause illness and deaths," Julia said. "And you do have your guests to consider."

The man with the jolly round face winked at Dave. "You've been coaching her, pal. I can tell that." He gave Julia a tolerant smile. "This fellow has you brainwashed. But even at that, you should realize the town has been here a lot of years and the hotel for half a century, and there's never been any trouble from polluted water yet."

"You're ignoring the fact that it's only in the past few years that the entire town of Wellsport has been linked with a community sewerage system and that all the waste material is drained into the cove at a spot not far from the hotel's disposal pipes," Dave said.

"Then it's the town's problem; not the hotel's," Malcomson said promptly. "You can't expect us to pay your service bills."

"I do expect you to show an awareness of what's happening," Dave said. "And in that way I can get some action from the Council."

The jolly face took on a more sober look. "I've got plenty to keep me busy at Manorview," the lawyer said. "You and the Council look after your own problems. If they built themselves a poor sewerage disposal system, that's their headache."

"The illness that results from it could be yours as well," Dave said.

The lawyer snapped his fingers and said airily, "We'll take our chances. You run the town, if you like, and leave Manorview to us."

Dave shrugged. "I warn you I'm going to bring this to the attention of the state health people. I'll tell them that both your system and the town's dump in the wrong area of the cove, much too close to the beach and the town. And I'll advise them that you have refused to give me any co-operation."

"That sounds like a threat!" All the good humor had left the round face, and his tone was now belligerent instead of merely boisterous.

"It's a statement of what I intend to do," the young doctor said. "Consider it what you like."

Both men had raised their voices again, and from the corner of her eye Julia could see that some of the people in the other groups sensed an argument was going on and were beginning to stare at them.

Apparently Steve Malcomson became aware of this at the same time as she did, for his manner underwent a swift change. He smiled and chuckled. "Well, now, Dave," he said, "you just go right ahead and do your worst. I suppose you have a right to a little excitement." He bowed to Julia. "Been a pleasure meeting you, Miss Lee. Maybe we can have a dance later, if this pessimist doesn't want to keep you all to himself."

Then, not giving Dave a chance to pick up the thread of the argument again, he went back to the group with whom he'd first been standing. Dave turned to Julia with a grim smile and sighed.

"What did you think of that?" he asked.

"I liked the way you stood up to him," she said.

"And I meant everything that I said," he assured her.

She nodded to the corner of the room where his mother was sitting. "I wish you could do as well where she's concerned."

He allowed a faint smile to cross his face. "Give me time," he said.

The music began again, and they danced. It turned out to be a pleasant evening after all. Julia wondered where Bill Dixon was. It was strange he hadn't put in an appearance. Then she remembered his conversation with the man on the dock the other day and supposed that he was seated at a table with some of his gambling cronies in one of the Manorview private rooms. It seemed a senseless way for him to waste his life.

It was inevitable that Julia should come face to face with Emily Farren at some point of the evening. It happened between dances when she was alone. Dave had gone downstairs to try to find Ned Berry, the mayor. The end of the dance had left her dangerously close to the corner Dave's mother and her friends were occupying, and now they had all gotten to their feet and were coming across the room to the exit. It meant Emily Farren would pass directly by Julia.

As Dr. William Farren and his wife came close to her, the doctor bowed his head slightly and smiled. It was a quiet greeting, but sincere and friendly. Emily Farren gave her a startled glance and then deliberately looked the other way.

When Dave came back upstairs, Edna Dixon was hanging on his arm. As the music began, she gave Julia a smile and said, "I'm going to have just a short dance with Dave. I haven't seen him a moment all evening."

Julia shrugged. "It's your party," she said quietly.

As they danced away from her, Dave's face was a picture of discomfiture. Julia watched them for a few minutes and then saw Steve Malcomson coming toward her with a broad smile on his jolly face. "I knew I'd be lucky if I waited long enough," he said. And with an exaggerated bow, "My dance, young lady."

"I'm glad you asked me." Julia smiled up to him as he whirled her out onto the floor. "I was beginning to feel like a wall-flower."

"A lovely flower," the lawyer corrected her; "never a wallflower. I saw Dave in the clutches of the lanky Edna and thought this might be my chance."

"She practically pulled him onto the floor," Julia said. "She has a very direct way."

The man with the jolly face laughed. "That's her trouble. She's too direct. In spite of her money and the fact she isn't bad-looking, she scares males off by the dozen."

Julia raised her eyebrows. "I don't mind, actually. She's entitled to a dance as our hostess. And I'm enjoying this one with you."

"Same here," Steve Malcomson said enthusiastically. "And by the way, why don't you try to talk some sense into Dave?"

"About what?"

"Bugging us at the hotel about this sewerage business. It's all nonsense, you know."

She smiled. "He might be right, although I hope he's not."

Steve Malcomson sighed in mock concern. "I can see you're loyal to little old Dave. Well, we'll just have to get at him some other way."

"Why not give him a fair hearing and see what he suggests?" she asked.

"Because it would cost us money and be for the town's benefit," the lawyer said. "That's the way it always turns out."

"And you're not willing to help the town?"

"Not one little bit!"

She shook her head in gentle wonder. "My, you're selfish!"

"That's exactly what I am," Steve Malcomson agreed happily. "I'm selfish and proud of it. It's the thing to which I credit all my success."

The music ended and the lawyer clapped heartily. Then he led her back to the spot where she'd been standing.

She said, "Even if you're selfish, you're an excellent dancer."

"We'll do it again sometime," he promised, patted her hand and moved off quickly. "Here comes Dave with murder in his eye. I'd better get on my way."

Dave came up to her. "What's wrong

with our legal friend?" he wanted to know.

Julia smiled. "He has an idea you're not too friendly disposed to him."

"I'm not," Jim said. "But I haven't any intention of starting a brawl."

"Now that your duty is done, we'd better leave," she said.

He made no protest, so they went at once. He saw her to the door and gave her a polite good night kiss, after making plans to pick her up and go to her father's on Sunday as usual.

Saturday night was quite a different occasion. Julia dressed in a smart new green evening gown with a strapless top. Bill Dixon was in a white dinner jacket when he picked her up, and he made no reference to the party the previous night or why he'd not been there. He seemed to be genuinely upset by the news of Colonel Morris' serious illness.

"No one around the hotel to replace the old boy," he commented gloomily. "He was a colorful character."

She found the dance at the Manorview House glamorous but a good deal quieter than the ones at the country club. For the most part, the group was older and there was not such a large attendance, since it was confined to guests of the hotel and not all the guests were dancers. Julia was impressed by the lovely evening dresses worn by the wealthy women and the mannered assurance of their white-jacketed escorts. The orchestra was the one that served the hotel and had been imported from New York for the season. Their music was understandably better than that provided by the local musicians who played for the country club, and she found it much easier to dance to.

During the mid-evening break in the music, she and Bill strolled out by the pool. There was a cool breeze, and he put his arm around her for protection.

"It also gives me an excellent excuse."

"We missed you at your sister's party last night," she said as they stood at the rail.

"Oh, that!" He looked out across the water. "I was busy here."

She looked up at him with a knowing expression. "Trying to even the score in that card game that goes on every night?"

Bill was startled. "What do you know about it?"

She shrugged. "Just that it happens. It must cost you a lot of money to gamble the way you do, and time as well. Doesn't it ever worry you?"

He gave her an amused look. "Now

you're starting to sound like my lawyer."

"You're so nice," she said, "I'd like to think you had no weaknesses."

"I've got plenty," he assured her with a smile. "But let's not worry about them. Karen, my little girl, will be here next week. I want you to meet her. That's the big news."

"I'm looking forward to it," Julia said.

"I'll phone you the day she arrives," Bill promised, "I'd like to have you come over to have dinner with us."

He was genuinely excited about Karen's coming. It wasn't hard to see the thing that counted above all else with Bill Dixon was his child. Julia liked him even more for this.

They went back to the dance, and when it ended Bill took her home.

Sunday was pleasant, and Dave took Julia up to her father's. He had to leave to visit Henry, the arthritis victim, who lived a mile up the road from Tom Lee. And there was a woman ill on a farm farther up the hill. By the time he made his calls and got back, Julia had dinner prepared. Since it was a fine warm night, they ate out on the verandah.

It was then that Dave launched into a re-cital of his troubles with the town Council and the hotel owners. Julia's father listened quietly until the young doctor had finished.

Then he said, "And they won't give you any sort of action?"

"They're just not interested," Julia put in.

Tom Lee looked from her to Dave with a puzzled expression on his face. "I'm just a poor old farmer," he said. "But I can see we may be heading for trouble."

Dave said, "They're not too smart. The season is pretty well over, and they may be lucky this year. But I'm not taking a chance on another season. I'm writing to the authorities in Augusta and presenting my views on the affair."

"That sounds the wisest way," Julia approved. "You've done all you can at this level."

Tom Lee lit his pipe. "Maybe I can do a little something."

Julia glanced at her father in surprise. It wasn't often that he bothered much about affairs in Wellsport, preferring to keep strictly to himself. But now, as he puffed thoughtfully on his pipe, she could tell the problem had caught his interest.

He said, "I'm on the committee of the local Dairy Farmers' Association. All of us

156

up on the hill here send in a little milk every day. I know I could get our secretary to draft a letter to the Council, if that would help."

"I wish you would," Dave said, looking pleased at the idea. "I'm glad you suggested it. Maybe I can get a few others to write as well."

Tom Lee smiled. "If their financial interests are not going to be hurt by a protest. It won't make much difference in our taxes up here, but you could have a hard time selling a new sewerage plant to the store owners on Main Street."

"I'll try anyhow," Dave said. And then to Julia, "We'd better get back earlier tonight. I have a few things at the hospital I want to check, and tomorrow is the day we take care of Professor Disher's cataract."

So it was agreed they go into Wellsport immediately after the meal. Tom Lee was sorry to hear about Colonel Morris' serious illness and took a keen interest as Dave described the operation they would perform on Professor Disher.

Then it was time to leave.

It was still bright daylight when they drove into the outskirts of Wellsport. Dave drove slowly, pointing out the various new motels and tourist cabins that had recently been built.

"In the past few years there have been at least a couple of dozen new ones," he said, "and right now they're nearly all full. It's fine for the merchants' pockets but hard on our health protection."

They passed a huge chain restaurant with pseudo New England architecture, including ornate white spires. The parking lot around it was crowded with cars, and there seemed to be a waiting line at the door.

Julia said, "That's only been open three or four years."

"I know," Dave agreed. "In the past decade, I'd be willing to bet our summer population has tripled." He drove down a winding curve where there was a wide bridge. It was the junction of a small river with the cove. To the left there was a camping area and trailer park with a few public buildings that had been hastily erected to give the transients a minimum of facilities.

The young doctor slowed the car almost to a stop as they passed this area. "Here's the worst hazard of all," he said grimly. "Everyone in this crowd swims in the cove. No private pools here, or private toilets, either. Get any kind of infectious disease going in this place, and there'll be a lot of sorry people in Wellsport."

Julia studied the rows of trailers and cars and the many small tents erected close together. "There must be at least several hundred people there," she said.

"The grounds are filled all summer long," Dave said, increasing the speed of the convertible to normal as they drove on into town. "They're making their profit on them now. I only hope there isn't a day of reckoning."

On Monday morning, Julia left Millie Randall at the desk on the second floor while she acted as scrub nurse for Dr. Dave Farren. Dave's father was assisting with the cataract operation, and Professor Disher seemed in good spirits about it.

Julia had visited him in his room earlier to give him a pre-medication so that he would arrive at the operating room in a suitably relaxed frame of mind.

The bearded little man smiled at her. "More treatment? They filled me full of happy pills last night."

She completed the injection and put the hypodermic needle on the tray. "This is just a last minute dose. How do you feel?"

"Right now I just want to get it over with," Professor Disher said. "I've got a lot

159

of painting I want to do."

Julia laughed. "Well, give yourself six weeks, and you'll be busy again."

He nodded, lying back on the pillow and relaxing as the drug began to take effect. "So many places I haven't done yet," he said. "A view of the cove from Rock Head. The covered bridge up on the Mountain Road. Never enough time to get around to them all. Never enough time." His voice became slightly thicker on the last words, and his eyelids closed.

She stood with him for a minute longer to be sure he'd fallen asleep, then quietly withdrew from the room. The next time she saw him, he was being wheeled into the brightly lit operating room. The team headed by Dr. Dave Farren were ready and waiting as the old artist was removed from the stretcher and lifted onto the operating table. Julia prepared the field of operation, and as Dave stepped forward she saw that it was nine-twenty-five.

It was a delicate procedure. A flap of the conjunctiva, the tissue covering the white of the eye, was carefully raised with scissors and dissected down to the edge of the cornea, the colored portion of the eye. The nurse anesthetist watched carefully as Dave worked. The professor's color was

160

good, and his breathing seemed normal. Dave was going about the procedure with calm precision, and his father did little but watch and make a comment from time to time.

Dave made an incision at the upper border of the cornea, and the iris, the muscle responsible for the eye's contraction and its color, was grasped with a forceps and a small section removed. He then took the entire lens in his forceps and slowly teased it out of the eyeball.

"Very neat," Dr. William Farren said tersely.

"No complications yet," Dave agreed. Now he was stitching the flap of conjunctiva back in place with tiny special sutures. Since the technique was so precise and demanding, Julia had been busy supplying minute instruments and sutures.

She felt a sense of elation at being part of the team that was restoring the old artist's eyesight.

Finally the attendants wheeled out the patient. He would be in bed for a week, and both eyes would remain bandaged for forty-eight hours, after which time the operated eye would be dressed. From then on the unoperated eye could remain exposed; the other one would have its dressings changed daily for the rest of the week.

Dave removed his mask and smiled at her. "He's in your hands from now on, Julia."

"He'll make a restless patient," Julia said, returning his smile. "Already he is planning to get back to his painting."

"See that his private nurse keeps him quiet in bed for at least four days," Dave warned. "We don't want to risk any hemorrhages or rupture of the stitches."

Dr. William Farren touched Julia's arm, his mild face showing admiration. "Dave is full of orders," he said, "and short on compliments. I was watching you as you worked with him. Dave is fortunate to have a scrub nurse like you."

With that the superintendent went out to the anteroom to change his clothes and wash up. Julia felt a surge of pleasure at the senior doctor's praise.

It was Dave's turn to look slightly embarrassed. "It seems I take you too much for granted," he said. "Remind me about that."

Julia's eyes twinkled. "I will," she promised.

She returned to the second floor and spent the last hour of the morning at her desk there. There were several new patients coming in later in the day, including a guest from the Manorview whom Dave was going to treat for a recurrence of arthritic pain. Jameson, the lobster fisherman, had improved so rapidly in his cast that he was ready to be discharged, although he would have to wear the cast as protection for his damaged disc for a short time longer. Julia explained that Dr. Farren would arrange for him to return to the hospital and have it removed.

The bluff old man chuckled. "Don't know whether I dare come in here again. You people might pounce on me and stick me in another bed."

But she knew he was pleased and satisfied with his recovery. She was about ready to go to lunch when the phone rang, and this time it was a personal call. Bill Dixon was at the other end of the line, and there was excitement in his voice.

"Karen arrived this morning," he said. "She's anxious to meet you. Can you come to the hotel for dinner with us tonight?"

"I'd love to," she said. "What time?"

"How about six?" Bill said. "She likes to eat early."

"Don't bother coming for me," Julia told him. "I'll be in the village anyway, and I'll walk over on my own."

Chapter Ten

When Julia arrived at the hotel that evening, Bill Dixon was waiting for her on the verandah by the front entrance. At his side was a serious-faced little girl with dark brown hair drawn back in a pony tail. Bill looked especially handsome in a summer suit of some light brown material, and the youngster was wearing a white dress with a good deal of crochet trimming that must have cost a fabulous amount. Julia was glad she'd chosen her best summer dress, a pink with lace trim and a flared skirt.

Bill gave her a smile of greeting as she came up the steps. "This is Karen," he said, his hand on the little girl's shoulder.

Julia shook hands with the solemn-faced little girl. "I'm glad to know you, Karen. My name is Julia."

Karen glanced up at her father for approval and then very formally said, "How do you do, Miss Lee."

Bill laughed. "I've been schooling her in that for the past half-hour." And then, giving Karen an affectionate pat, "You may call her Julia if you like."

The small freckled face broke into a surprisingly bright smile. "Hello, Julia."

"That's more like it," Julia said. And glancing around at the gardens, which were filled with strolling guests: "My, it's lovely here tonight."

Bill looked pleased. "Manorview offers nothing but the best," he said. "We'd better go in, as I've reserved a table."

They sat at a prominent table in the big dining room, not far from the orchestra. Julia was impressed by the interest Karen showed in the dinner music. Now that the ice was broken, she lost most of her reserve and talked almost continually. She liked her school in Florida, and she also liked playing the piano and being a member of the junior Red Cross. It went on endlessly.

After dinner they went out to the back verandah and sat in a spot that gave them a view of the pool and the golf course. It was so pleasant and peaceful Julia couldn't help envying the people who had money enough to come there season after season and enjoy the many attractions Manorview offered. Far out across the water, pleasure craft passed by, and it was so clear she could even make out the details of the marking buoys.

Bill sat with them for a while and then excused himself when a phone call came for him. Karen now gave all her attention to Julia.

The bright, questioning eyes studied her. "You're a nurse, aren't you?"

"That's right," Julia agreed.

"I'd like to be a nurse," Karen said. "Will you show me your hospital?"

"I'll be glad to!" Julia smiled. "We haven't many children patients just now, but you'll find lots of interesting things there."

Karen sighed. "I'm glad my Daddy likes you. You're nice."

Julia blushed. "Thank you. Your Daddy has a lot of friends."

"I know." The small head with the tight pony tail turned as Karen studied the swimming pool. "But I don't like most of them. They talk all grown up and don't pay any attention to me."

"Well, I'll give you lots of attention," Julia promised. "I like little girls, but I don't know many."

Karen turned to her. "Why don't you come to Florida with us?"

"I have a job here," Julia said. "Maybe I'll go down for a visit one day."

"Would you, really?" Karen's small face

brightened again. Whenever she smiled, she had an extra touch of elfin charm.

Bill came back and sat down again. "Sorry I had to leave," he apologized. "It was a business call. Looks as if I'll have to go into Portland tonight."

"That's too bad," Julia said. "It's so lovely here."

Bill looked uncomfortable. "I won't be leaving for a while," he said. "And Karen has to go to bed early."

"Oh, no, Daddy!" the little girl protested, and took his arm in both her hands.

He smiled at her. "I'll take you for a drive first. We'll drive Julia home."

"There's no need to," Julia said at once.

But Karen was happy again. "Oh, yes!" she exclaimed. "I'd like that."

So it was settled. And Bill went across to the parking lot to get his car. This time Karen went with him, her small hand holding one of his. Julia was to wait for them to come back and pick her up. She stood watching them stroll down the gravel walk in animated conversation. She was glad Bill had Karen; she was sure he needed his little daughter badly.

"Karen is a little doll, isn't she?" It was Edna Dixon who said this. She had come up beside Julia.

Caught off guard, Julia turned with a smile. "Yes, I like her."

Edna was wearing a smart yellow dress that suited her. She eyed Julia curiously. "You've been seeing a lot of Bill lately."

Julia shrugged, feeling it was none of the tall girl's business. "We have been together a few times," she said.

"It seems like a lot of times to me." Edna smiled in an arch manner. "I take it you're interested in my brother. I thought you were Dr. Dave Farren's girl."

Julia could scarcely believe her ears. She hadn't expected Edna to be so brazen. She said, "Dave and I are good friends."

"His mother seems to think it's more serious than that," Edna said.

"I hardly know his mother," Julia answered.

"Then I take it that Dave is not promised," Edna went on in her teasing voice. "You won't resent it if I see him occasionally?"

Julia barely controlled her anger. "That's entirely up to David."

The tall blonde girl tossed her head. "I hope I haven't offended you," she said with a superior smirk, and went inside.

Bill came back with the car, and Julia put the whole matter out of her mind.

Karen sat between them and talked steadily all during the drive. She made Bill stop at the canteen by the trailer camp so she could buy herself a soft ice cream cone.

Bill shook his head and smiled. "We have gallons of ice cream at the hotel, but that doesn't suit her. She has to buy it here!"

Julia was sympathetic. "I think it's the fun of getting out of the car and standing in line with the other children she enjoys more than anything else."

Karen was still enjoying her cone when Julia got out of the car. She left them, promising to see them soon again. And she told Bill he could bring the little girl to the hospital any time he liked.

Julia went to bed early that night, and next morning reported back on duty at the hospital again. Professor Disher was feeling quite well after his operation but complaining about the bandages on his eyes. When Julia made her first round of calls, she stopped to chat with the old artist for a few minutes.

"You mustn't be impatient," she reminded him. "And we mustn't have you fussing around in bed too much. You don't want to injure your eye."

"I thought the doctor had it fixed already," Professor Disher said plaintively.

"Dr. Farren did an excellent job on your eye, but too much motion could ruin the delicate stitches, and then you'd be in real trouble."

"But he only operated on one eye," the old artist said. "Why do both of them have to be bandaged?"

She laughed. "So there'll be no strain on the one we've taken care of."

Professor Disher sighed. "I'm sick of this darkness."

"Just rest," Julia told him, and winked at the young red-haired nurse who was specialing him. "You have a good-looking nurse to do everything for you."

"Doesn't make any difference what she looks like," the artist said bitterly. "You've fixed it so I can't see her."

Assuring him he'd have to put up with the bandages only for a few days, Julia moved on to the other patients. Several of the new ones had not yet had their medication charts properly completed. To do this she had to wait until the various doctors came. Dr. Daniels was due back in town, and she had an idea he might come to the hospital earlier than usual. She hoped that he would, as she wanted to question him about his gall bladder case.

Dave was the first to put in an appearance and make a quick visit around the floor. He had just come back to see Julia at the desk when the elevator opened and Dr. Daniels hobbled out.

Julia took one look at his face and knew that he was in a depressed mood. The veteran doctor painfully made his way over to them and addressed Dave.

"The colonel is dead," he said heavily.

Dave frowned. "I'm not surprised. When did it happen?"

"Yesterday," Dr. Daniels said, "before they really made any thorough tests."

"There wasn't much need for them," Dave said with a sigh. "I haven't a doubt that he had a malignant brain tumor. And it was probably much more advanced than we realized."

Dr. Daniels nodded his bald head, the wizened face clouded. "I've lost a good friend. So has the town. He'll be missed here."

"No doubt about that," Dave said.

The old man gave Julia a small smile of greeting. "I've been ignoring you, Miss Lee. Didn't mean to. I must have a look at my patients now that I'm here." And before she could reply, he turned to Dave again. "There is something else. I have a sick child

171

at the trailer camp who's worrying me."

Dave showed interest. "Oh?"

"I've been seeing her for a week," Dr. Daniels said. "She's camping there with her family for the month of August. At first it seemed just a simple summer upset. But there was a message for me this morning that she was worse. Could you arrange to meet me after lunch and see her? I'd like another opinion."

"You say she's at the trailer grounds," Dave said. "That doesn't seem a good place for a youngster as sick as she must be. Hadn't you better have her brought in here?"

The old man shrugged. "I suggested that. But the family panicked. They're a close group, and this is a strange part of the country to them." He paused and then added, "Also, I have an idea they're worried about the expense."

Dave frowned. "I know. That's always a problem with these people." He seemed to make a sudden decision. "Why can't we go there before lunch, as soon as you've finished seeing your patients here?"

Dr. Daniels showed mild astonishment. "I suppose that would be all right."

Dave was plainly troubled by the case.

"What have been the main symptoms she's shown?" he asked.

The veteran doctor thought a moment. "Well, she didn't seem too ill at first. She had some fever, nausea and headaches. She complained of the headaches."

Dave asked him tersely, "Any nosebleeds?"

Dr. Daniels gave him a strange look. "I'm surprised that you mentioned that. I'd almost forgotten. Yes, as a matter of fact, her mother said she'd had several minor nosebleeds."

Dave's face became more grave, and Julia was certain he suspected something much more serious than Dr. Daniels guessed. However, he said nothing.

She gave Dr. Daniels a questioning look. "Would you like to make the rounds now, Doctor?"

He nodded. "Yes. May as well get it over with. I won't be long, Dave."

The young doctor nodded. "I'll wait."

Julia didn't have a chance to speak to Dave privately until they came back to the desk where Dave had sat down to do some paper work.

Dr. Daniels was busy giving Millie Randall some specific instructions about the care of the arthritis case from the hotel.

Julia knew it would probably be her only chance to speak to Dave alone before he left.

She said, "You seemed upset about that case at the trailer camp."

He looked up at her with a sober face. "I'm almost afraid to go over there."

"You think it's really serious?"

His jaw took on a grim line. "Unless I'm very far wrong, Dr. Daniels' little girl is the first victim of our water pollution."

"Oh, no!"

"Let's hope I'm wrong," he said quietly. "I'll see you as soon as I come back."

Julia watched him leave with the old doctor and found herself trembling. She knew it was ridiculous to be so concerned about a situation about which there was no certainty. But all the weeks during which Dave had been harping on the danger of the cove waters had built up tension within her. She expected the worst!

Julia worried all through the lunch hour. She found she had no appetite and took only a little soup and some plain bread and butter. She was taking a phone call at her desk when Dave returned shortly after one o'clock. One glance at the young doctor's tense face as he emerged from the elevator told her all she needed to know.

She finished the call and put down the receiver. Then she got up and faced him. "What's the verdict?"

He bit his lower lip as he hesitated before answering. Then he said, "I'm not sure."

"How is the child?"

"The fever is worse," Dave said. "She's terribly ill. Her temperature is 105 degrees, and she is in quiet delirium."

Julia gave a small gasp. "That sounds almost like —" She left the sentence unfinished.

He nodded slowly. "All we need now are rose spots on the abdomen and chest, and we'll know we have a first class case of typhoid fever."

"What are you going to do?"

"The child has to have hospital care at once," Dave said. He glanced toward the east corridor. "I want you to empty all the rooms at the end of that corridor and seal it off halfway as an isolation ward."

Julia assented. "There'll be no difficulty. All the rooms are vacant except one. That's the arthritis case. He can be moved."

"Very well," Dave said. "Until we're certain what we're up against, you must use sterile technique. And on no account are the nurses looking after the little girl to take care of any of the other patients."

"I understand," she said.

"Once we're sure," he went on grimly, "I want everyone on the staff to be given a vaccination."

She looked at him with frightened eyes. "Surely it won't be that bad."

His face was a stern mask. "It could be a lot worse than you imagine. If this is the first case of an epidemic of typhoid, heaven help this town!"

He turned abruptly and headed for the elevator again. Julia watched him go, standing there for a full moment after the elevator doors had closed. Then she roused herself to action.

She decided to take just one person into her confidence: Millie Randall. She cornered the stout girl in the supply room and explained the emergency. Millie's eyes became wide with fear.

She asked, "Do you honestly think it's typhoid?"

"The symptoms are the same," Julia said. "The child's only been ill two weeks. The third week is the most dangerous one."

"What happens then?" the stout nurse wanted to know.

"You should remember." Julia smiled grimly. "It's in all the nursing books. In the third week you can get complications of hemorrhage and perforation. If the bleeding is severe, you get anemia. If perforation occurs, you get severe pain, shock and acute peritonitis."

Millie went pale. "Sounds delightful! Do I get the job of looking after her?"

Julia shrugged. "No. I can't spare you. I think I'll use Jane Freeman. It seems to me she had a vaccination against typhoid when she made that trip to Europe last year."

The stout girl nodded vigorously. "She did. I remember her telling us."

So it was settled that Jane Freeman should look after the isolation area. The ambulance brought the child in, and Dr. Dave Farren went to the room and stayed with her. Not long afterward Dr. Daniels appeared. He came directly to Julia and asked, "How is it going?"

She shook her head. "I don't know. Dr. Dave Farren is down with your patient now."

The old man glanced down the corridor, his hands working nervously. He gave her a penetrating look. "You know what it may be?"

"Yes."

177

"What about the other staff members on the floor?"

"They are aware we're preparing to look after a contagious case," she said. "They don't know the details." She paused. "I'm afraid it won't be possible to keep it a secret long."

Dr. Daniels gave a deep sigh. "I don't expect so."

Just then Dave came striding down the corridor toward them. He came up to Dr. Daniels and said simply, "The reddish spots are in evidence. There's no longer any doubt! Typhoid!"

The old man passed a gnarled hand over his eyes. He gave a small moan. "I should have known," he said. "I should have realized sooner."

"Don't blame yourself," Dave said angrily. "You and I are victims. The ones who bear the guilt are the Council and the Dixon crowd."

Dr. Daniels seemed to have aged in a matter of minutes. He sank into the empty chair by Julia and looked up at the young doctor with a pitiful expression on his time-ravaged face.

"What's to be done?"

"I'll tell Dad first," Dave said. "Then we can see about giving the staff vaccinations." He slapped his fist in the open palm of his other hand. "The trailer grounds! Everyone there will have to be vaccinated. The place will have to be closed at once! And the child's family should be isolated until we're sure none of the others are already infected."

Dr. Daniels touched a hand to his temple. "We'll need vaccine and help. I'll call the G.P. at Lincoln. He'll do what he can, I know."

"And I'll have my father get the official help we'll need from Augusta," Dave said. "We'd better go down and see him right away. I'd rather have you with me when I tell him the case is definite. It isn't going to be an easy moment for him."

A half-hour passed, and tension mounted on the second floor. Even the patients were aware of something vague and disturbing in the air, and Julia and the other members of the staff were hard put to give them answers. The word from the little girl's sick room was grave. Jane Freeman reported that her patient was deep in delirium.

When Dave returned to the floor, he was alone. He stopped at the desk and sighed. "I'm staying up here for a while. If anyone wants me, send a message down to the room." He gave Julia a meaning look. "I'm expecting visitors."

They weren't long in coming. And Julia was not surprised when she saw Mayor Ned Berry and the Dixons' lawyer-manager step off the elevator. Ned Berry's owlish face was a green color, and his eyes showed fear behind the horn-rimmed glasses. Steve Malcomson's jolly round face had taken on a peaked look. There was no sign of a smile this afternoon.

The lawyer spoke first. "Dr. Farren asked us to come here. Dr. Dave Farren," Malcomson added by way of explanation.

"I'll let him know you've arrived," Julia said, and sent the message down by a nurse.

Dave came promptly. Julia knew that he must have been anticipating this moment. She bent over her desk and pretended to be absorbed in her charts, but as they were standing within a few feet of her, she was able to hear what they were saying in spite of the low tones in which the discussion was conducted.

Dave's voice was low but severe. "I hope you two are satisfied now that we have an epidemic on our hands."

"Don't talk like that, Dave," the mayor implored.

Steve Malcomson showed more annoyance than fear. "Why blame us? Likely these people brought this thing with them, didn't get it from the cove water at all. There's always some kind of sickness in those trailer parks!"

Dave apparently hadn't missed the note of disgust in the lawyer's voice. He said, "Typhoid hits the rich just as easily as it does the poor. Maybe one of your hotel people will be next, and that will spoil your theory."

"What are we going to do?" the mayor asked anxiously.

"All the things that should have been done before," Dave said sarcastically. "Only now there'll have to be mass vaccination as well, isolation for any people suspected as carriers, and all the rest of the safeguards necessary when you are faced with a threatened epidemic."

"One sick little girl!" Steve Malcomson exploded angrily, his voice rising. "You're causing all this fuss over one sick child!"

"And if she dies," Dave said calmly, "I'll think of you and Ned as her murderers."

"That's not fair!" Ned Berry bleated. "I'm only the mayor. The other members of the Council have the say!"

"You ignored everything I told you," Dave said. "Now we have to face the consequences."

"Mass vaccination will throw all Wellsport into a panic," Steve Malcomson argued. "You'd serve the people better if you kept this thing quiet. Once it gets out, the town will empty overnight. I won't be able to keep a guest at the hotel!"

"You should have thought of that sooner," Dave said.

"But does there have to be publicity?" the mayor pleaded. "Not only will it hurt business in the town now, but we'll be suffering from it for years to come. Things like this can ruin a summer resort."

Dave said, "That gives me a certain amount of satisfaction."

Steve Malcomson snorted. "You're doing this deliberately. You've wanted this to happen."

"Don't say that," Dave warned the lawyer angrily, "or I may forget I'm a doctor and where we are and let you have the beating you deserve."

Julia's phone chose that moment to ring and break up the little drama that was being played a few feet behind her. When she picked up the receiver, she recognized Dr. Daniels' voice.

The old man seemed agitated. "Is Dr. Dave handy?" he asked.

"Right here," she said. "I'll put him on the phone." And she called Dave.

She stood by while he talked with the old doctor. The mayor and the lawyer stood silent and ashamed, neither of them looking her way. The conversation on the phone lasted several minutes. When Dave put the receiver down, he turned to Julia first.

"You'll be having a second patient for the contagious ward," he said with a meaningful glance.

She nodded. "Will the patient be arriving soon?"

"Dr. Daniels is bringing him in now." Dave turned to the two waiting men and said coldly, "Well, gentlemen, there's your answer."

Mayor Ned Berry gave him a harried look. "What is it, Dave?"

"Dr. Daniels has confirmed another typhoid case."

"Probably got it from the girl," Steve Malcomson blustered. "She'd naturally endanger everyone at the trailer camp."

"This case isn't at the trailer camp," Dave said. "It's on the other side of the town, in the big new motel. This man has

183

never been near the trailer camp. But last week he swam in the cove every day!"

Mayor Ned Berry's voice broke. "We're ruined! The whole town's ruined!"

"That's not the worst that can happen to you," Dave sternly reminded him. "You run as good a chance as anyone else of landing in a bed of feverish agony with a typhus ulcer eating out your insides!"

Chapter Eleven

Any prospect of hours off or shift work was out of the question now. The entire hospital was placed on an emergency basis. Julia stayed on duty all through the day and into the evening. Dr. William Farren, the superintendent, had set the wheels in motion for anyone in the area who wanted to be treated with vaccine to attend depots that had been established in the hospital, the fire station and the schoolhouse. Some of the nursing staff were on hand at these centers, and there were also volunteer workers from the various community groups.

When Julia called Sarah Thomas to tell her she wouldn't be home at the usual time, she found the matronly woman unusually excited.

"Is it what they are saying?" she asked. "Typhoid fever?"

"There are at least two cases," Julia admitted.

"I remember it from the old days," the woman at the other end of the line said sadly. "It's a terrible sickness."

"We'll have to hope that we caught it in time to avoid any spread," Julia said.

"That's true enough," Sarah Thomas declared. "There must be something I can do."

Julia hesitated. "They could probably use volunteers at one of the depots. You could ask at the fire station."

"I'll do that," Sarah Thomas said emphatically. "I'll go there right now."

Dave spent a lot of his time with the two cases already in the hospital. Dr. William Farren paid occasional visits to the floor, looking haggard and shaken. The girl at the switchboard told Julia the press and other news media had been continually interrupting him with calls. One reporter from Augusta had already arrived on the scene and was covering the situation for a national news syndicate. The story had already been on radio and television and would be in all the evening papers. Wellsport was getting the kind of publicity it could well have avoided.

The convalescing Professor Disher probed Julia when she visited him. "They tell me there's an epidemic in town," he said. "I hear dozens of people are sick and some dead."

She smiled at the old man. "You're

giving full sway to your imagination. Nothing so dramatic has been happening."

His tone was querulous. "Don't treat me like a child. There must be some truth in it. The whole hospital is upside down."

Julia sighed. "For a patient with his eyes completely bandaged, you manage to know a good deal!"

Professor Disher sounded hurt. "I depended on you to tell me the truth."

"I will," she said. And she gave him a full report, ending with, "So you see it isn't as bad as you thought."

The old artist made an unhappy sound. "Just my luck! I had to miss all this!"

"I'd say you were fortunate," she told him. "You're safe here. Who knows but what you'd have gotten the fever?"

"I never catch anything," he said testily. "But I'd like to paint someone with it. You know, in the last stages, like those old masters! Those fellows in the sixteenth century could produce a painting that let you know what a plague was about!"

Julia shook her head. "You're nothing but an egotistical old man! And I'm not going to encourage you by discussing it any more."

She went back to her post at the desk. And she stayed there until nearly ten. It had been arranged that she go home then and that Grace Perkins would come on duty two hours earlier. The relief shift regular, Laura Britt, had been sent to one of the vaccine depots, so they were bridging her time.

As Julia got off the elevator downstairs, she ran into Dave. As they stood facing each other, he looked at her with concerned eyes and said, "You're tired! It's written all over you."

"I've been on duty since seven this morning," she reminded him.

"I know," he said in a worried voice. "I'll see if I can arrange for you to report late in the morning."

"Don't!" she protested. "I'm needed and I'll be here."

"It won't help any if you make yourself ill," he told her.

"I'll be all right."

He hesitated and then asked, "Would you like a cup of coffee? The cafeteria is open, and I thought I might have one."

She looked into his anxious face and knew that he wanted her to join him. And even though she was tired, she decided that she should. If it had been a difficult day for her, it had been doubly hard for him.

She smiled. "I think some coffee would do me good."

So they found themselves in a booth in the deserted cafeteria, over large cups of steaming coffee. Dave lit a cigarette and sat back in a relaxed mood.

"I helped for a while with the vaccinations here," he said. "You should have seen the collection we got, all of them looking frightened and only taking the needle because they thought the alternative might be worse."

"It's good a lot decided to take advantage of the vaccinations," Julia said. "It will cut down the risk of spread that much."

He nodded. "We had them from the camping grounds and a surprising number of the bluebloods from Manorview House. It was funny seeing them standing in line together. Disease is certainly a leveler." He paused. "You want to hear the prize funny story of the day?"

She knew it must be ironic by the expression on his face. "Go ahead," she said.

"My thoughtful mother phoned Dad and insisted that he make a special trip home to give her and Edna Dixon a shot of vaccine!" He shook his head grimly. "What a sweet, unselfish pair those two are! No standing in a public line for them!"

Julia shrugged. "At least you won't have to worry about them."

"I'm worried about Dad," Dave said angrily. "He's working under terrible stress. The newspapers are giving him a bad time as well!"

"In spite of all your warnings," she said, "it doesn't seem possible."

"I know," he agreed with a sigh. "It is a kind of a nightmare. I didn't anticipate typhoid myself — a disease so rare nowadays that some medical students never see a case right through their internship."

"But there's no doubt?"

"None," he said. "It's not so unusual as that. A summer resort in Scotland had a bout of it last year. They traced it to tainted meat from South America. It spread some, and quite a few people died."

"When will the crisis come here?" Julia said, studying his tired face.

He considered the question with arched brows. "Probably the next ten days will tell the story. The little girl is desperately ill now and the male patient almost as bad. Both of them were well advanced before we found out their trouble."

"Are there any medications that help?"

Dave nodded. "Luckily, we're living in the age of antibiotics. Penicillin and the sulfanilamides are useless with typhoid. But we do have aureomycin and cholomycetin. Both these drugs have a marked effect."

"Then the disease isn't the killer it used to be."

"We can be thankful for that," he agreed. "But people still do die of it."

Julia gave him an admiring look. "I thought you handled the mayor and Malcomson wonderfully."

"There wasn't much satisfaction in it," Dave said. "I'd have been a lot more pleased if they'd listened to me in the first place."

"Now they'll have to do something."

"That's the only good thing we can expect to come out of this," he said. "They'll have to put in a new sewerage system now. But it will cost them more than just paying for the improvements. Tourist business in this area will suffer for a long time to come."

"I can imagine that a lot of people changed their plans about coming here when they heard the news."

"And those who are here are leaving as fast as they can," Dave said grimly. "I'll bet by the end of the week the Manorview will be empty."

"They can only blame themselves."

"There's some satisfaction in that," he said, finishing his coffee. "I'll drive you home."

"No. I wouldn't think of it." She rose in protest.

"I'm leaving for a few hours anyhow," he said, getting up with a wan smile. "I can use a little sleep, too."

He let her off at her door. They kissed good night in the car. They were both tired and in a subdued mood.

The following day two more suspected victims were brought in. Dr. Daniels hobbled off the elevator much earlier than usual and spent most of the day at the hospital. The town was full of rumors.

Millie shook her head as she told Julia, "My mother wouldn't listen to me. She really believes every room here is filled with typhoid cases and that we have patients in beds in the halls."

"You should make her come and see for herself," Julia said. "These silly rumors will scare people into becoming ill."

"I know," Millie agreed. "She says nearly fifty people have died already from it. I tried to tell her there hadn't been a single death yet, but she wouldn't listen to me."

Julia sighed. "I suppose some of the

192

town gossips are having a field day with this."

"They never miss a chance!" Millie said gloomily.

The added strain on the staff soon began to tell. Julia found herself more jumpy and irritable than usual. The patients seemed to pick up the general tension and so they, in turn, were more difficult. Only Dave seemed to be able to carry on without any noticeable change in his regular manner. His square young face showed lines of weariness, but he behaved normally in every way.

It was after lunch on the fourth day of their ordeal that Julia got the first of two surprises. The elevator door opened, and her father stepped out. He was wearing what he called his town suit, a drab gray woollen of winter weight. He looked warm and uncomfortable in it, but he approached her with a smile.

"Got a drive in," he said laconically.

She said, "You're reversing the process. Most people are getting out of town."

"I like to be different," he admitted.

"So that's why you're here," she said.

"No. But I heard they were looking for volunteer workers. Figured there might be something I could do."

It was typical of him. Though he normally shut himself off from the community, he was available to it in time of trouble. She was touched by his sincere desire to help.

"I doubt if there are any jobs open," she said. "Too bad you aren't a nurse. But go downstairs and talk to Dr. William Farren about it. I'll phone down and let him know who you are."

Tom Lee smiled. "Do I look so bad I need a recommendation?"

"Not a bit of it," she assured him. "But he'll take more interest if he knows you're my father. And I want him to know that I have a handsome parent."

Her father chuckled. "That desk job sure has made you a diplomat!" And he went downstairs.

He didn't come back, but she heard later that he was helping clean up over at the trailer camp. The place was clear of people now, and town employees were gathering up any debris around the place and burning it. So Tom Lee had found a spot where he could be useful after all.

Dave came by with his report on the little girl who'd been the first one struck down by typhoid. "The antibiotics are helping," he said. "At least there are signs of her fever lessening and not so many periods of delirium."

"Then she does have a chance of pulling through," Julia said.

"I hope so," Dave said. "It's too early to tell about the others. But the new cases are milder than the first ones."

Julia's second surprise of the day came via a phone call. When she picked up the receiver, she recognized Bill Dixon's voice. In the hectic confusion that had followed the outbreak of typhoid, she realized she'd almost completely forgotten him.

His voice sounded strangely different. "I'm afraid I'm in serious trouble," he said.

She was at once concerned. "What is it?"

"Karen. She's ill. Has been for several days. I tried a few home remedies, as I didn't want to take her to a doctor's office with all this typhoid around." He hesitated. "She's not getting any better."

"What seems to be troubling her?" Julia asked, picturing the solemn face of the little girl and trying to keep her voice calm.

"She has a fever and headaches and now —" he paused — "well, she doesn't seem quite rational. I can't get to her at all!"

"Bill!" Julia spoke sharply. "Bring her here at once!"

"No!" he protested. "I can't risk taking her over there."

"There's no risk, and you know it!" Julia spoke wearily. "Stop lying to yourself, Bill. You know what's wrong. She has it!"

There was a short silence at the other end of the phone. Then Bill answered in a dull voice, "I'll come with her now."

Julia was there when he brought her in. He carried her tenderly in his arms and protested when they took her from him. Dave went to Karen's room as soon as she was admitted. Julia had no more than a glance of the familiar dark hair over the top of the blanket Bill had wrapped around the child.

Julia showed him to the waiting room and stood there as he paced up and down.

"If anything happens to her, I'm finished," he said.

"Dave will look after her," Julia tried to comfort him. "You should have brought her here when it first happened."

He stopped his pacing and gave her a pitiful look. "You know why I didn't. I was afraid. I knew what it was. But I didn't dare admit it."

"The others at the hotel must have guessed. What did Edna think?"

"Edna!" His voice was filled with disgust.

"She wouldn't even come near Karen's room. I've looked after her alone since the first night." His eyes were bright with fear. "And now she doesn't even know me, Julia! She hasn't been able to recognize me since early this morning."

She went to him and took his arm. "Delirium is part of it," she told him. "It doesn't mean she's in any worse danger than before. In fact, a high fever is sometimes helpful."

He spoke without looking at her. "I feel so guilty. I wouldn't listen to Farren. And the night before she took sick, I left her to go to the races at Scarborough Downs." He shook his head. "If she gets over this, that's finished."

Julia said, "There's every chance she'll be all right. No one has died yet, not even the first little girl who came in so very ill."

Bill looked at her. "I heard otherwise. One of the porters at the hotel said about twenty people have died from it."

Julia showed annoyance. "That's all scare talk. We've heard that it's going on, but there's nothing we can do to stop it."

Bill shook his head. "I should have come to you first. But I've been almost crazy!" He sank down into a handy chair and, cov-

197

ering his face with his hands, began to sob like a small boy.

When the tears lessened, she patted him on the shoulder. "You'll feel better now. I'll go and get you some coffee."

When she came back with a tray, Dave was there with him.

"Karen is a terribly sick little girl," Dave said, "but there's not a reason in the world you should consider her condition hopeless."

Bill searched Dave's face with anxious eyes. "You're not telling me that to keep me quiet?"

Dave shook his head. "There'd be little point in that. I'm not saying she isn't in danger. She is. But the present outbreak hasn't ended in a death so far. I consider that encouraging."

"The others are all recovering?"

Dave corrected him gently. "Holding their own as yet. I'll be satisfied if Karen does the same."

"I feel so helpless," Bill said, and stared at the floor. "Guilty, too! I listened to Malcomson because I wanted to. I should have known you were telling the truth."

"This is no time to discuss that," Dave said.

"I can't get it out of my mind," Bill said,

raising his eyes to meet Dave's. "I feel personally responsible."

Dave's strong young face betrayed no emotion. He answered quietly: "If we take that attitude, there's none of us without blame. The important thing now is that Karen and the others recover."

Bill nodded. "I can't bring myself to leave her. Can you rent me a room here?"

"I'm afraid that isn't possible," Dave said. "We're pressed for space as it is. And it would hardly be fair to make an exception in your case. Karen is going to have the best of care. And you can come back whenever you like."

"Thank you, Doctor." The young hotel owner showed embarrassment. "I shouldn't have asked."

"No harm done," Dave said. "And now I'll have to go back."

After he left them alone, Julia poured Bill some coffee and sat with him while he slowly drank it.

At last, looking somewhat more like his regular self, Bill stood up and, with a note of apology in his voice, said, "Forgive me for keeping you this way. I forget the business of the hospital has to go on."

She smiled. "You are part of our business right now. Feeling better?"

"A good deal," he said. "I'll go back to the hotel and come here again after dinner."

"That sounds like a good plan," she agreed.

He started for the door and then paused to turn and say, "Julia, that doctor of yours is quite a guy."

Julia nodded. "I know," she said softly.

She went with him to the elevator and stayed until it came. When the door opened, Steve Malcomson stepped out. The ruddy features had crumpled into an expression of bewilderment.

He came to Bill quickly and said, "I just heard. I thought there might be something I could do."

Julia found herself caught up in the drama of the confrontation.

At last Bill answered in a quiet, dry tone. "Thank you; everything is being looked after." And he got into the elevator and stood with his eyes studying the floor until the door closed.

Steve Malcomson's mouth was agape. He turned to Julia. "Well, that was cool enough," he said in a complaining tone.

"He's not himself," Julia reminded the lawyer. "It isn't fair to expect too much of him under the circumstances."

The round-faced man was still nursing his hurt. "All I tried to do was help."

She couldn't resist giving him a meaningful look and saying, "Maybe he thinks it's a little late."

Malcomson's face crimsoned. "A whole summer's earnings at the hotel down the drain," he said angrily. "And now this!" He gave the elevator button a savage push.

The business of the hospital continued at its usual rate. The typhoid threat had brought things to a stop as far as the town was concerned. There were no summer tourists left, even the hotel having been emptied. But the normal number of births, deaths, accidents and illnesses occurred among the local population, and Dixon Memorial had to cope with these in addition to handling the typhoid cases.

One thing about the epidemic encouraged them all. There had been no deaths from it thus far among the more than half-dozen victims in the isolation ward. As each day passed, they became hopeful that the lives of everyone struck down by the epidemic might be saved. The girl who had been entered first was making a slow but heartening recovery, and there had been no new cases reported for a week. Dave had privately expressed his opinion to Julia that there would be no others.

Then the situation reversed itself with frightening rapidity. The adult male case was suddenly seized with very severe abdominal pains. Dave lost no time in contacting Julia.

"He's perforated," he said grimly. "Only one thing we can do now. Operate. Get the O.R. ready."

Julia had not acted as scrub nurse since the beginning of the typhus epidemic. Now she found herself under the lights of the pale green room facing an entirely new surgical problem.

Dr. Daniels was assisting, and as soon as Dave opened the patient the old man gave an exclamation. "The entire area is infected," he said. "Advanced peritonitis!"

Dave worked doggedly cleaning the field and suturing the hole in the intestine caused by the typhoid ulcer. Julia began to breathe easier as the operation neared completion.

The first indication that they were still in trouble came from the nurse anesthetist. She spoke sharply. "Dr. Farren! The patient's respiration is poor!"

The next few minutes were a nightmare. Dave made every effort to revive the man on the table. But it gradually became clear to all of them that the typhoid had undermined his system to the point where he could not survive the operation. It was exactly eight minutes later that Dave tore off his mask.

"He's gone," he announced in a dull voice. There was a frozen silence in the room. The typhoid epidemic had claimed its first victim.

Chapter Twelve

Word of the patient's death spread quickly through the hospital and the town as well. Faces that had begun to show relief at once became gloomy again. Bill Dixon came over to the hospital and paced worriedly in front of Julia.

"I thought the danger period was over," he said.

"Not yet," she told him. "But this was an especially severe case. Dave says he thinks all the others, including Karen, are doing well."

The tall man shook his head. "I won't have an easy minute until I see her on her feet again."

Julia advised him, "Don't let this panic you. I'm sure she's going to be all right."

It was more a hope than a true feeling of assurance. But, as it turned out, the death in the operating room had marked the low point of their fortunes in the battle with the epidemic. All the other patients in the isolation ward showed a steady improvement.

Perhaps Julia's happiest moment came when Bill Dixon arrived to take Karen home to the hotel. He seemed full of his old cheerfulness again, and when he stopped with the solemn-faced youngster to bid Julia goodbye, his face was positively radiant.

"I've hired a practical nurse to be with Karen a few weeks," he told her. "We'll be staying on at the hotel until late October."

Karen looked up at her wistfully. "You'll come to dinner again, won't you?"

Julia knelt by the youngster. "Of course I will!" And she gave the child a big hug and kiss.

Bill Dixon laughed. "Almost sells me on the idea of being a patient."

Julia stood up. "Don't jump to conclusions. We have an age limit for this kind of treatment."

His handsome face became serious. "You will accept Karen's invitation, I hope. We both owe you so much. There are a few of the staff here until we close, including a chef. So I can guarantee a true Manorview meal."

"That's enough enticement to make me come," Julia joked.

She saw them to the elevator, and once again she was thankful for her vocation.

For her there was nothing that matched the satisfaction of helping restore suffering people to health. She felt privileged to even a minor role in this important phase of living.

The isolation ward was closed, and the hospital returned to its normal routine. Professor Disher came back for a brief check-up, wearing his new glasses.

"Don't mind them," he told Julia. "Now that I've gotten used to them, I think they give me a sort of dignity."

Julia studied the dapper little bearded man. His beret was at its usual, jaunty angle, and even though the Maine weather was getting cooler, he still wore his dark Bermuda shorts. It was true the glasses did suit him.

"I wouldn't worry about contact lenses," she advised. "I think you're right. These suit you very well."

Professor Disher chuckled. "Should have had them years ago. But I'm vain, you know. I've been reading and doing some painting every day. And on Monday I'm going back to teach."

"What about your other operation?" Julia asked.

"Dr. Farren says he thinks it can wait until next summer," the old artist said.

"And that suits me fine. I'd like him to do the other eye, too."

She laughed. "You'll be missing a couple of years of Down East painting."

He shook his head. "Don't have to do that. I've got the images of most of the scenic spots around here planted on my memory. I'll paint between times at the college."

"It is a lovely area," she said.

"My favorite," Professor Disher said seriously. "There's something special about the rugged coastline of Maine. I'd like to spend a winter here sometime."

"You'd find it severe," she warned him.

"The snow scenes would make up for that," the old man said with a smile. "Maybe I'll come down for a few days during the winter holidays."

The country club had cut down its activity during the typhoid scare and, with the summer population gone, had given up their dances altogether.

As a result Dave and Julia didn't see much of each other outside hospital hours for quite a period. Bill Dixon phoned her repeatedly, and she went over and had dinner with him and Karen. It was a pleasantly relaxing evening, and they ate in one of the small private dining rooms. Afterward they strolled around the deserted grounds. After Karen went to bed, Julia sat with Bill before a blazing log fire in the big stone fireplace in the main lobby.

They sat back on the comfortable divan and discussed many things. The epidemic was already almost forgotten, and they talked mostly of the future, although Bill did make a reference to the new sewerage plans.

"The hotel has already approved the new plans," he told her. "They're starting work on an extension in a few days."

"I'm glad it's settled," she said. "Each year seems to bring larger crowds here, and the improvement is long overdue."

He frowned. "It took a hard lesson to make most of us realize that. But at least now it's being done."

"The tourist trade will build up again," she said. "It may take a little time, but people will come back."

Bill sighed. "I hope so. We're not geared for too many losing seasons." And with a smile: "I'm not too worried. I doubt if it's possible to resist the charm of Maine or its people for any length of time."

"As a native, I'll accept the compliment." Julia laughed.

"I mean it sincerely," he said. "I think I'd

come back here even if I didn't have the hotel."

"I know what you mean," she agreed. "I think I'd feel the same way."

The flaming logs cast a flickering pattern on his handsome face. His eyes met hers. "Just what are yours plans, Julia?"

She gave a small shrug. "I don't suppose I have any. I'll go on nursing at Dixon Memorial."

"I mean your personal plans for the future," he said. "You must have something in mind besides your profession."

Julia stared into the flames. "I used to think I had it all settled. Now I'm not so sure."

Bill said, "I take it Dr. Dave Farren played a large part in them."

"He did," she admitted. And then, correcting herself, "He does."

The man beside her was silent a moment, and then, with a heavy sigh, he reached over and took her hand. "That doesn't surprise me. I think you couldn't do better, though I wish you'd consider a second offer."

She turned to him. "I didn't realize I had one."

"You do," he said gravely. "Karen isn't the only one who'd like to make you part of the family. I'd be honored if you'd marry me, Julia."

She studied his serious face for a long moment. "I think you'll make a fine husband, Bill. I wish I could be more certain about myself, my own feelings."

"There's no rush," he said. "Think it over carefully."

"I will," she promised.

He took her in his arms and kissed her gently. Then they sat for a long time watching the logs burn out. At last there were only embers and ashes left, and Julia rose to leave. Bill drove her home and seemed reluctant to leave as he stood with her on the verandah.

"You'll be over again," he said. "We'll be staying another week at least."

"I'll try," she promised.

He kissed her good night and, with a final wave from the roadway, got into the car and drove away.

Julia watched the red tail lights vanish at the end of the street with moist eyes. She had the feeling that they wouldn't be seeing each other again, at least for a long time.

She went inside, her mind a turmoil of thoughts. She adored the elfin charm of Karen and admired Bill a great deal. In

210

spite of his wealth, he was a lonely man with many problems, including raising his little girl without the aid of a mother. Had things been different, she would have been overjoyed to accept the offer of marriage he'd made her. Instead, this moment of intimacy tonight had brought her only sorrow and doubts.

She was confused. For such a long time she had been in love only with Dave. Dave had been the one man she'd thought of until her meeting with Bill Dixon. Until this summer, Bill had been just a remote figure, the wealthy playboy who owned the Manorview House, and to whom she'd never even talked. But he'd revealed that he'd taken notice of her even when she was a waitress during her school holidays. She had caught up with him in time, so that he now found her desirable as a wife.

It was flattering, especially since she was so fond of Bill. But she wouldn't want to marry anyone unless she was sure. There was no question in her mind that she loved Dave in a deeper, more intense way. But there were many problems to be settled. She was convinced that his mother would never warm to her. And Julia couldn't help disliking Emily Farren. She distrusted her motives and felt she was a much different sort of person from Dave. Yet it was only natural that the young doctor should have strong feelings of loyalty toward his mother.

And there was the question of Dave's professional future. Would he curb his ambition and be content to stay on at Dixon Memorial? She knew this was Emily Farren's wish. It fitted in with her social ambitions as the leader of the Wellsport social colony. She was ready to sacrifice Dave's larger opportunities to perpetuate her position as the large frog in the ridiculously small pond. Julia knew she couldn't stand by and let this happen, at least not as Dave's wife. She would feel she'd become a collaborator in a plot against him as a person.

What it meant was that she couldn't marry Dave under present conditions. She'd never feel ready to marry him if he stayed on in Wellsport. It would be too little to be his wife and have Emily Farren manipulating the puppet strings of their lives. Unless Dave showed some resolution on his own, there was nothing for them. Her love could only turn to bitterness.

She turned off the bedroom light and lay back against the pillow. She stared up into the darkness for a long time. Perhaps she should think more seriously of Bill's offer.

She felt she could bring him at least a measure of happiness, and it would be a joy to have Karen as her own, see her grow to the lovely young womanhood of which she already showed promise. Many marriages had been built on less and thrived long and sturdily.

But there was that possible moment when Bill might look into her eyes and in his quiet way ask: "Do you really love me, Julia?"

And she wouldn't be able to answer with any degree of sincerity. She wouldn't be able to make him properly understand the complexity of her feelings. In the end she'd make him suffer through the knowledge that she'd entered into a marriage with him because she couldn't see a way to find happiness with a man she loved more. With a sigh, she turned on her side and tried to sleep.

The following morning she had to make a visit to Dr. William Farren's office. There were some records that she wished to transfer to the main billing division.

The mild-mannered superintendent took the papers and smiled at her. "We haven't had many opportunities to chat, with all the pressure of the past few weeks."

"I know," Julia agreed. "But I think things are settling back to normal now."

Dave's father sighed. "I certainly hope so. Dave and I are going to be keeping bachelor hall for a while."

"I hadn't heard," she said, at once interested.

Dr. William Farren nodded. "Yes. My wife is going to Europe for a month or two. She and Edna Dixon are making the trip together."

It was the first time Julia had heard Edna's name mentioned in some time. She knew that Bill's sister had left Wellsport the day after Karen had been admitted to the hospital.

"They are meeting in New York," the doctor went on. "Of course it's not Emily's first trip overseas, but she likes to go every once in a while to keep up with the changes there."

"I can understand," Julia murmured. She was certain that Emily would return with a huge collection of slides and spend most of the next year giving cultural talks to any and all of the various Wellsport groups. Yes, she'd certainly make the most of the trip.

The senior Dr. Farren eyed her humorously. "So if we get tired of our own cooking, maybe Dave can persuade you to come over and whip up a meal for us."

214

She laughed. "I might be a disappointment." At the same time she appreciated his saying it and the spirit of friendliness behind their talk. She was sure that the somewhat henpecked man wanted to let her know that he approved her.

"You were a tower of strength during the crisis," he said, rising. "I know that Dave has a great deal of confidence in you."

"We all are proud of your son," she said. "I've considered it a privilege to work with him in surgery."

Dr. William Farren gave her a knowing look. "You've seen quite a lot of him outside hospital hours as well."

She smiled. "I have enjoyed his company."

"Good!" The senior doctor smiled in return. "Keep an eye on him. He leads a strenuous, lonely life. He can use good friends."

Julia left Dave's father, certain that he had deliberately led the conversation to his son to let her know that he was worried about him and would welcome her help. It gave her a warm feeling to know that at least one of the young doctor's parents was on her side.

Millie Randall was at the desk when Julia returned to the second floor. The stout girl got up, saying, "There's a message for you from Dr. Daniels. He wants you to call him at his office."

Julia did and found the old man had resumed his traditional gruff manner. "Got a patient for you. Coming in this afternoon," the veteran doctor said. "Gastric ulcer. It's Matt Higgins from over Lincoln way. We've had him in before. This time it looks like an operation. I'll talk to Dave about it."

Julia promised to have everything ready for the patient's admission. It was like old times again, with a steady flow of patients. She helped Jane Freeman with an intravenous that had proven difficult; interviewed several of the other patients on the convalescent list and noted changes in their medication and diet. Just before lunch time, she helped Millie Randall move a patient who was in traction.

When she entered the cafeteria, she saw Dave sitting at the table where they usually met. He stood up, and she went over to him.

He smiled. "Decided to treat myself to waitress service today."

After they sat down, she told him about Dr. Daniels' call. He remembered the patient.

Julia said, "Dr. Daniels plans to have you look at Mr. Higgins. He seemed to think he will need an operation."

"I know his history," Dave agreed. "Likely Daniels is right. The old man usually is."

She laughed. "He sounded as cranky as ever this morning."

"He's talking about retiring," Dave said. "But he never will, unless his arthritis finally gets the best of him. Doctoring is his life."

"I know," she agreed.

They ordered, and Dave continued to discuss hospital matters. She waited for him to mention his mother's vacation, but he made no mention of it.

Halfway through lunch, he looked up suddenly and said, "By the way, we're going to have a new doctor in Wellsport."

She was surprised. "When?"

"He's coming in a month or so. Has a practice in Pennsylvania he has to wind up before he makes the move here."

"Is he a general practitioner?" Julia asked.

"That, and a surgeon as well," Dave said. "Dad knows him by reputation and has been trying to get him interested in Dixon Memorial for some time."

"We could use another doctor in the area," she said. "It will make it easier for Dr. Daniels."

"I know." Dave nodded. "He'll be able

to confine himself to his old patients."

She thought she should mention her conversation with his father at this point. "I hear," she said, "your mother and Edna are heading for Europe."

Dave seemed not too interested. "I guess that's the plan."

"Did you see Edna before she left?"

"No. Not many people did. I understand she has a phobia about infectious diseases. And I suppose Karen coming down the way she did upset her."

"I suppose so," Julia agreed. She felt the discussion was not getting anywhere so she dropped it.

Over coffee, Dave said, "We've been missing out on our Sunday visits with your father since the epidemic. How about this weekend?"

"Fine," she agreed. "I've been neglecting him."

"Should be a nice drive up the mountain," he said. "This is the time of year the trees begin really to change color."

Dr. Daniels arrived with his ulcer patient, and Julia became absorbed in the dozens of details that went to make up one of her days as head nurse on the second floor. Later, when she went home, she thought about her conversation with Dave again and anticipated the visit with her father on Sunday. The chances were that Dave would leave them alone while he made his regular call on Henry, the old man on the farm above who was bothered by severe chronic arthritis. She hoped to have a few minutes to talk with her father. She was feeling confused and lost.

It worked out as she'd thought. The drive up the winding country road was a treat. Most of the leaves had changed to crimson and orange, making the countryside a blaze of color. There was a sharp tang in the air, but the sun was bright and the day ideal.

Tom Lee had bought a large roast of beef when he heard they were coming, and Julia at once settled down to get it prepared and in the oven.

Dave looked at his watch. "I'd better go up and check on Henry. Then I'll be able to sit back and relax."

"Why don't you?" she agreed, feeling a little guilty in her anxiety to send him on his way.

As soon as she and her father were alone, she went over and sat by his chair. Tom Lee put down his paper and smiled at her.

"What's the problem, honey?" he asked. "I could tell you had one from the moment you arrived."

She laughed self-consciously, making a pattern on her apron with her hand. "Am I that easy to read?"

"No," Tom Lee said. "But somehow a man understands his daughter. I'd like to hear about whatever is bothering you."

She told him.

He nodded gravely. "It's a turning point in your life. We face them all along the way. And it's the choices we make that decide our way of living. Every now and then you have to ask yourself what is right, what is important!"

"I know." She sighed. "Sometimes it's hard to be sure."

Tom Lee smiled. "None of us is ever able to make all the right decisions. But we can try. Many people make wrong ones and live with them all their lives. It's one of the most difficult aspects of our existence."

"I just can't make a choice, not as things are," she said.

"Even when we refuse to choose a path of action, we're adding to the pattern of our lives," her father said. "We can't help ourselves. You know what Thoreau says: 'Things do not change; we change.' "

Julia got up, moved across to the screen door and stood looking out at the amber of the autumn sunlight on the lawn and trees.

"Perhaps I should marry Bill," she said at last.

"I don't want to advise you," her father said. "What's come between you and Dave?"

She turned to him. "Didn't I make that clear? His mother and his lack of ambition."

Tom Lee's weathered face took on a smile. "If anyone can be accused of a lack of ambition, I suppose it's me. I gave up a teaching career and came here to farm."

"That was different," she said. "This is the sort of life you wanted."

"Perhaps Dave prefers to stay here as a general practitioner in a small town," Tom Lee said. "I think you should discuss it with him again before you make any rash decisions."

So she said no more on the subject, but went back to preparing the roast while her father returned to his paper. Shortly afterward she heard the sound of Dave's car coming up the gravel driveway.

He came in with a smile. "It's a wonderful afternoon. Haven't you finished with that meat yet?"

She closed the oven door. "It's done now."

Dave said, "Let's go for a walk. There won't be many days left like this to enjoy."

Julia took off her apron and started toward the door. "We'll be back soon."

Tom Lee smiled. "Don't hurry on my account. And don't worry about the roast. I'll keep an eye on it."

It was perfect outdoors. Julia took Dave along a road running out back of the farm. It was an abandoned private road that hadn't been used for some years. Some of it had been grown over, but it remained open enough for easy walking.

The tall trees formed an arch overhead, and from time to time there was the call of a bird or the quick rustle of some small unseen animal in the undergrowth.

"This is certainly primitive enough," Dave said.

"It's more fun than the highway." Julia smiled at him. "I often used to come here alone when I was living at home."

He eyed her with some surprise. "I hadn't tagged you as the aloof type."

"I am," she said, "especially when I have problems. I used to come out here and try and think out anything that was bothering me."

"Did you come often?"

She stared up at the trees as they moved along. "Often enough."

"Too bad I didn't know about this

222

place," he said. "I could have used it during these past weeks."

There was something about the way he said it which caused her to look at him. "Have you been having problems?"

"All sorts," he said. "But they are settled now."

"You make me curious," Julia told him.

Dave laughed. "Maybe that's what I want, Julia. I've decided to leave Wellsport."

She stopped and stared at him. "You have?"

He smiled. "Don't look so shocked! I thought that was what you wanted me to do."

"Yes, but — well, I don't know what your plans are."

"I've been offered a fellowship in surgery at a prominent Boston clinic," he said. "It will mean two years with little pay but plenty of experience. When I've finished, it should qualify me to do the special type of surgery I want."

Julia's eyes were bright with happiness. "I'm so glad, Dave! I know it's what you should do."

He shrugged. "My mother doesn't think so. And my father isn't sure. But at least he doesn't try to make my decisions. He's even helped by getting this doctor from

Pennsylvania to come and take over for me."

"That's what you were trying to tell me the other day," she said.

Dave nodded. "I intended to tell you everything then, but decided it wasn't the right time or place."

"I'm glad you waited until now," Julia told him.

"There's just one other thing," Dave said. "On my application to the clinic, I told them I was being married, that I'd have my wife with me when I went there. It could be awkward if I showed up without one."

She looked up at him. "Don't worry about it," she said softly.

Then they were in each other's arms for a kiss that lasted a long time and made up for all the weeks of doubt and indecision. Julia felt secure at last. She knew this was right for her. But there was still one disturbing factor.

As Dave released her, she said, "There's still your mother. She doesn't like me."

"I wouldn't worry about it," Dave said. "Let the future take care of it. I've heard being a grandmother works wonders with difficult women."